I0551828

# Kinky Little Secrets

## Sexy Stories Collection

VOLUME 45

10 EROTIC SHORT STORIES

BREANA KOHR

Publisher's Note: This is a work of fiction. Names, characters, places, and incidents are a product of the author's imagination. Locales and public names are sometimes used for atmospheric purposes. Any resemblance to actual people, living or dead, or to businesses, companies, events, institutions, or locales is completely coincidental.

Kinky Little Secrets/ Breana Kohr. -- 1st ed.
Xplicit Press, an imprint of TLM Media LLC

ISBN-13: 978-1-62327-576-1
ISBN-10: 1-62327-576-8
eISBN: 978-1-62327-626-3

Printed in the United States of America

# CONTENTS

# 1 OUR SEX SLAVE

Amelia. What a beautiful name, what an insane little girl! Now don't get me wrong, Amelia was an attractive woman, in her mid-twenties, and with dark brown hair and unsettling, passionate and yet very playful eyes. She had a thin body and a squeaky voice—the type of girl you wouldn't think twice about approaching in a bar.

To be honest, when I first met Amelia, I was impressed. She had a nice way with words and a very congenial personality. That's her parasitic way, you see. She charms you, promises the world, and then moves in for the kill.

Now I'm not saying she's literally or physically dangerous. But she is the type of girl to drive you slightly bonkers.

When did the whole Amelia thing start? The whole thing started with an act of kindness. Amelia had started talking to my girlfriend, having met her at the supermarket. You have to understand that Amelia is very outgoing...to a fault, to a major fault. She has little dignity and insists on unburdening her problems upon anyone she meets. So as soon as she saw how kind of a person Kitty was, she pounced.

"You poor thing!" Kitty remarked, honestly buying Amelia's stories.

"Yes, I know. My roommate has ordered me to come up with $1,000 dollars within two weeks or he is kicking me out to the curb. I guess I'll have to sleep on a bench; unless of course, I can raise $1,000. I'm pretty sure I can make $500 on the Internet within a week. But to be honest, the second week worries me."

"Oh?" Kitty listened in confusion, as Amelia proceeded to babble on about GooGoo Adwords and some complicated strategy to make money off "clicks". This was lie number eight by Amelia, the first of several hundred to come.

Kitty was perturbed about the poor girl's fate, and horrified at her origins, which Amelia insisted upon sharing to anyone who would listen.

"So her step father is evil and is trying to kill her?"

"That's what she told me. I think Amelia's kind of nuts!" Kitty said with a shrug.

"You know I didn't think so at first. But the more you tell me, I'm starting to think she's a bit goofy. I mean some of her stories contradict each other. That's the first sign of a chronic liar."

"Yeah."

Kitty and I tossed and turned in bed. "Still...I don't think she's lying about being stranded out there on the street. I can definitely see her roommate kicking her out for being annoying, if not completely broke."

"Hmm. I guess so."

"But what do we owe her, Jack?" Kitty asked in worry. "We just met her. Sometimes she seems nutty...but sometimes she seems like a regular girl who's just down on her luck, you know?"

I turned over and looked into the eyes of my beloved girlfriend, her flowing brown hair, and her adorable bangs. She had the perfect voluptuous shape and a beautiful, earnest smile. The compassion in her eyes was apparent whenever she looked, whenever she spoke, and whenever she reached out to people. And she was never sexier than when she was naked, natural and looking into my eyes.

"I don't know. I have thought about letting her stay here. But I decided not to say anything to her for sure until I asked you."

I shrugged and shifted a bit uncomfortably. "The thought did cross my mind. But...I don't know. Isn't that a risk? What if she is a psychotic and has a meltdown?"

"Yeah, I know."

"But...what's the worst that can happen. I suppose it's not any more volatile than having your crazy sister come over and visit."

"That's true!"

"And I know I hate doing dishes. I suppose we could offer Amelia temporary lodging, just until she gets back on her feet."

Kitty's eyes lit up; as always, she was so relieved to be doing the right thing.

Jack lay asleep one night thoroughly exhausted, as I studied his cute and endearing face. He had a wonderful glow about his skin, and dark hair that accentuated his dark eyes and broad facial features. He was so sexy, but in that subdued, sophisticated sort of way. Whether he was sporting a suit or just walking around in pajamas, he always set the room on fire. And yet...he looked so stressed that night.

Oh Jack, how was I supposed to know letting Amelia live here a few days was such a big mistake? My poor hubby had been furious for the past few days, as our house has become a mess. There were dishes packed to the ceiling and trash all over our once neat living room! The only thing that had changed is that Amelia is now crashing here, and when I say crashing, I mean crashed, as in beached and inactive. She mostly lies on the couch and watches TV, or hogs the XXXBox 180 console.

Jack did not ask for much. All he asked was that she cleaned up after herself and chipped in with the housework. But every time we mentioned something to Amelia, the stories begin.

"I can't do it, today. I am having Lupus complications and am immobile."

"You have Lupus? Since when?"

"Since yesterday, I made a self-diagnosis," she said with a completely straight face.

And if it's not a crippling disease, it's another farfetched scenario.

"I had $100 to give to you. But I believe a maintenance man entered our apartment and stole it."

"But...you were here all day?" an annoyed Jack asked.

"Apparently he confiscated it while I was in the shower. I heard distinctly Mexican voices out in the kitchen. It is really shocking that they would stoop so low."

And my favorite…

"I can't work today. I am honoring the Sabbath, as I take my Jewish heritage very seriously."

"I thought you said you were Buddhist?" I asked tiredly.

"I am a Buddhist Jew. I am a Jew by ethnicity, but a Buddhist in faith. But my faith and race intermingle and thus I observe traditions of both."

Later, Jack and I fumed in our bedroom, exchanging crazy Amelia stories.

"She never wants to do any work. Heaven forbid she lift a finger to help us out. Now I'm practically raising a child in addition to supporting a family."

I sighed. "And she has no plans to leave, apparently. I tied to broach the subject again but she said—"

"Let me guess," a furious Jack interrupted. "She's allergic to the sun!"

"Actually…she claims she's saving up money so she can go be with her Internet hermaphrodite 'boyfriend.'"

"What?"

"That's what she claimed last I talked to her."

"Then tell him or her, or it, that we'll drive Amelia ourselves if he'll take her off our hands!"

"The latest news is that they are on a

break."

Jack groaned, and we rolled over and fell asleep.

The entire dynamic between us changed when I caught Amelia using the computer late one night.

I walked over to the computer desk in the living room to see what the hell Amelia was laughing about at three a.m. As soon as she heard me coming, she frantically clicked the mouse, as if to hide something. Oh great, I thought. What, is she hacking into a bank website or something?

"What are you doing?" I asked as I approached the desk.

"Nothing!" Amelia replied frantically, trying to close the window. Ah, if only my computer weren't so anxious and full of spyware.

I saw exactly what she was doing.

The first window was a YeeHaw instant messenger box and Amelia was talking to BigJohntheStudd94. The second window was an erotica story from some free porn site. I almost laughed out loud the moment I realized she was plagiarizing cybersex for her virtual guy friend.

"Are you having cybersex?"

"No, no, no," she exclaimed still trying to click the window. "Damn this window!"

she muttered. "It's not what it looks like. I was actually doing a report, a psychological report on virtual relationships for a news magazine."

"Uh huh," I asked suspiciously as I read parts of her transcript. "So saying you want to 'feel a big cock in between your legs'?" That's part of the report?"

"Well," she tittered away. "No, that's just me goofing off. But the report is real. It is due by eight a.m. actually."

"Amelia!" I couldn't help but laugh, playing the disciplining parent to my surrogate bad child. "You should be ashamed of yourself," I said with a grin. Having cybersex at night...when you should be sleeping for your big job interview."

"What?"

"You know? The job interview you claimed you had yesterday? At 10 a.m.?"

"Oh right, that. Well, that fell through. It turns out the guy doing the hiring was an anti-Semite."

"Amelia that is such bullshit. You're not even Jewish."

"Absolutely I am! My birthday certificate proves it."

"Whatever."

"Unfortunately, it's lost somewhere in California in my old house. I buried it to protect it from my evil step dad—"

"Amelia, just stop talking. I'm tired of

the lies."

"But it's the truth."

"All I know for sure is," I said with a smirk, "Is that you're a little YeeHaw instant messenger slut. You're using my Internet time and my computer to have cybersex with some guy..."

I read the transcript again.

"And apparently a guy that's not even your boyfriend."

I found Amelia's eyes and looked down to emphasize my victory.

"No...This is just for a report I'm writing."

"Amelia...do you want to stay here?"

"I need to stay here," he mumbled. "I can't afford to leave yet."

"Then I want you to admit, right now, that you're an Internet slut."

"What?"

"Do it. Say it."

"But I'm—"

"Amelia, I am kicking you out the door right now if you don't tell me what I want to hear. And Kitty's not going to do a damned thing, because she is at her wits end. I am giving you one more chance. Now say it. "I am an Internet slut"."

Amelia looked up at me, all out of options, and respecting my determined visage.

"I am an Internet slut."

"Good girl." I stared at her another

moment, making sure she got the point. I excused myself and bid her goodnight.

I didn't hear anymore typing. I think my little comment was good punishment for that bad girl. It's about time she learned some respect for other people.

I listened to Jack's humbling story in unhealthy fascination.

"You made her say that?"

"Yeah. Well, it was to prove a point, is all. I wanted her to admit that I was right and she was wrong. And no lie she came up with could change that."

"But that's not what you made her say," I said with a head tilt. You made her say, 'I am a slut'."

"Well...I guess so."

I laughed at the thought. "And the fact that she did it is really funny."

"Maybe she is a slut."

"And does that appeal to you? The idea of having a house slut?" I giggled.

Jack chortled at the notion. "Well, a sex slave at least contributes something to the household. Damn Amelia just takes up space."

We turned and rolled over in our beds, trying to forget the silly conversation and go to bed.

Jack couldn't sleep and started

following his abstract and deviant thoughts, to see where they led. "Of course...it's a perfect solution to our dilemma. We can't get rid of Amelia...and she doesn't contribute anything. If we made her our, you know, 'sex slave' then it would probably force her to leave and go out on her own."

"Huh," I replied, shocked I was even considering his halfhearted fantasy. "You're right that would probably force her to leave...or...at least do whatever it is we asked."

"Like what?" Jack laughed, and had a mad gaze in his eye. "So let's do it. Let's just pretend to go through with it. We scare Amelia away for good."

I laughed hard, not taking the idea seriously quite yet. "Or we inherit a sex slave. Who knew I would get a sex slave for my birthday present?"

"Oh, she's not going to do it," Jack dismissed. "It's just to rattle her...scare her straight, maybe."

"Okay," I finally said with a nod, psyching myself up to play the part. "Let's do it. We both talk to her tomorrow. Or shall I tell her?"

"You tell her. Just...you know, have a little fun with it. The more 'fun' we have, the more she'll want to get the hell out of here," Jack snickered.

"Okay. I will then." I smiled at the

delicious thought.

The next morning I walked out to the living room to find Amelia snacking on chips and watching TV.

"Hey Amelia," I started innocuously. "I think I want to draw. I need your assistance."

"But I'm watching this."

"It's not a request," I said glaring into her eyes, and startling her up from the couch.

"What do you need?" she asked sheepishly.

"I want to go back to my roots. One of my favorite things to draw is the female figure."

Amelia gulped down her nervous feeling and stood still, stunned at my request.

"Take your blouse off," I said eyeing her white and blue housedress with a banded waist and lace crochet neckline.

"Why?" she asked blankly.

"I want to draw you in your bra."

"But..." Amelia laughed in disbelief. "Isn't that a little weird?"

"I don't think so," I said coldly. "It's my house. You're living here because of me. And if you want to eat tonight, I suggest you do what I say."

She looked at me in surprise and folded

her arms, trying to think her way out of a puzzling dilemma. For once, the truth and her lies were all irrelevant. This time it was all about my will. She was powerless to resist.

"Does Jack know about this?"

"Why?" I laughed. "Do you think Jack is going to protect you? Honey, you have no idea what Jack is thinking about you right now. You know he told me about your little Internet slut escapade."

Amelia listened, her eyes becoming wider, as fear gripped her.

"Is that what you are, Amelia? A little slut?"

"No...I'm not."

"So do as you're told. Take off your shirt and show me your bra."

Amelia thought it over. She reluctantly grabbed her sleeves and lifted the shirt over her head, tossing it to the floor. She protruded her chest, showcasing her white pointy bra, hiding her perky breasts from view.

My heart rate pounded as I saw Amelia face me and await new orders. I couldn't believe Jack's wicked idea had backfired! I felt a surge of erotic energy build within me, and pondered the possibilities.

Amelia waited, eyeing me in sourness, but perfectly willing to do whatever I commanded, just to keep a roof over her head. It felt wrong to me...but it felt so empowering.

"I can't really see anything, darling. I want you take off your bra. And show me your breasts." I said it low-toned, almost a mutter, because of my excitement. Amelia glared me down but followed my directions, and unfastened her bra giving me a full and open view of her natural floppy breasts.

I walked up to her slowly, looking at her bare breasts and then back to her blushing face. "Kiss me," I whispered.

She didn't encourage it, she only tolerated it. I reached out and kissed her on the lips. She stood still at first, but then let me invade her mouth with my curious tongue. She jumped slightly when I put my hands on her nipples but then relaxed, letting me explore her body with my fingers.

"Is that all?" she pouted, as I released the embrace.

"No, that's not all," I said curtly. "You take that tone with me, young lady, and you're going to get punished. Do you understand?"

She avoided my eyes and nodded to the floor.

"Take your panties off, Amelia. I want to see your hairy crotch."

Amelia sighed and tried to resist the thought. "This is sexual harassment, Kitty!"

"You don't work here. Slut. If you don't like my request then get the fuck out of my house."

"Fine," Amelia griped as she pulled her panties down showing me her brown pubic hair. "Does Jack know you're a lesbian?"

"Shut up. I will say when I want to hear from you. You know the call...I'll say speak, puppy, speak."

"Can I go now?"

"No. Spread your legs a little."

She groaned again, but obliged me, opening her snatch. "Hold it open."

She pulled her labia lips apart and showed me her clitoris. I bent down and sat on my knees so that I could get a closer look.

"That's a pretty clitty," I said with a sneer. I wet my index finger and touched it, listening closely to Amelia's soft sighs. I played with her big clit a few more seconds and then put my finger up her snatch. She was dry down there at first, but after a few licks from my own spit, I got her pussy wet and slippery.

"How does that feel?"

"Mmm...hmm-hmm..."

I rubbed it down faster, enjoying listening to her heartbeat race and feeling her pussy becoming wetter as the moments passed. Before she could climax, I ended her game, amused at my talented fingers and very curious about my girl's equipment.

"Okay. You've earned your freedom. At least for today."

I stood up and walked away, not bothering to say another word to our new house slave.

"Wow," I said with a long smile. "I'm sorry I missed that."

"It was amazing. To have full control over another person's life...to humiliate her...to play with her like a doll. God, I've never felt anything like it, honey." Kitty said, honestly surprised at herself. "Does this make us slightly sick?"

"I don't know. Who the hell knew Amelia would go along with it?"

"Do you think we're taking advantage of her?"

"We?" I asked with an evil little grin. "Seems to me you got all the fun so far, when do I get to play with our new little toy?"

Kitty laughed a good sport. "Whenever you want. She's not just mine. She's ours, honey."

I giggled myself to sleep, just thinking of how much fun I was going to have tomorrow.

"Oh sweetie?" Kitty reminded me with a

tender kiss. "You know I love you so much."

"I love you so much, hon."

"You know nothing you do to Amelia counts. Right? I want you to enjoy your day off tomorrow."

"Yeah, I know. Thanks baby." I kissed my beloved on the cheek.

Kitty went out grocery shopping by the time I arrived home. As usual, I found Amelia spaced out on the couch wearing her bra and panties without permission. Leave it to Amelia to be a lousy sex slave in addition to a poor houseguest.

I figured I should tidy up the messy home first, wash dishes and put away my files. After I finished, I walked up to our houseguest and made a request.

"Stand up."

"I can't see the TV."

"Stand up, Internet slut."

Amelia groused at me. "Not you too."

"Darling...do you have any idea of what I could do to you?"

"You can't do anything. Shit, I'm sick and tired of you and Kitty treating me like a slut slave."

"I don't care. Guess what? I looked through your bag last night. I found baggies of marijuana. You know it's illegal,

17

right? I could turn you into the cops right now. Is that what you want?"

She thought it over and prepared for the worst. "No."

"Maybe I should be generous. How about I just take your drugs away from you?"

"No..." she said firmly. "I need them."

"You need them to what? Relax after a stressful day on the couch?"

"I—"

"Shut the fuck up."

She silenced quickly and made me feel like a king. I already felt my erection busting through my pants.

"Take off your bra and panties, Amelia."

"I'm going to tell, Kitty," she said bitterly, pulling off her undies yet again for our viewing pleasure.

"That's up to you, honey. If you keep this a secret between us, I will be gentle. If you say anything to Kitty, I'm going to make sure it hurts."

"What?"

"This..."

I swatted my hand across Amelia's naked ass and shivered with anticipation.

"What are you doing?"

"I'm spanking you, stupid. What does it look like?"

I swatted her again, making sure her ass cheeks got red as a rose.

She hissed and suspired, probably

wanting release. Maybe a virgin, or at least a celibate for a few years.

"Do you want to me to fuck you, slave?"

"No," she quickly replied.

"Then I won't. But you still have chores to do."

"What?" she growled, losing patience.

"Spread your ass cheeks. I want to look at your tight little asshole."

She shut her eyes in disgusted defeat.

"Do it. If you want to be a good little girl, you're going to follow the rules."

She looked at me lazily and turned her back to me, spreading her ass cheeks wide for my prurient interest.

"I'm going to put my finger up there. Are you ready?"

"Yes..."

"Yes, master. Say it."

"Yes..."

"Yes what?"

"Yes, master."

"You're such a good girl, Amelia. I always knew you were a good, obedient girl," I said warmly as I felt around that warm, tight anus. She sighed deeply, feeling an equal measure of humiliation, discomfort and, dare I say, unexpected ecstasy.

"Uhhnnn..." she breathed deeply, feeling the penetration and the steady rhythm I was building. I pressed down, finding the cul-de-sac through the backdoor and enjoyed her guttural hymns reacting to my experiment.

She almost climaxed, but I let her go to fight another day. Before I excused her, I ordered her to give me a hug like a good little girl. The hug was warm, inviting and a bit of a squeeze...just like her tight little asshole.

"Do you think we're being too hard on Amelia?" I asked Jack.

"I don't know. Do you?"

"I can't tell anymore," I said worriedly. "Sometimes I don't know when to stop...the game...it's like I can't pull the brakes sometimes."

"Me either. Then again, we've never had a willing house slave before."

"Some of the things I've done to her, Jack, they're so humiliating. I don't know what the hell I was thinking asking her to do those things. But my god, I can't seem to control myself. Every time I'm around her, I want to play with her...corrupt her. What's wrong with us?"

"Maybe...maybe it's time to be nice to her for a change."

"You think so?"

"What would Amelia like that she's not already taking from us, rent-free?"

"Love, acceptance, maybe a night on a

comfortable bed for a change rather than the couch?"

"Then let's let her sleep on our bed," Jack said confidently with a strong nod. "Let's give Amelia something she deserves for a change."

Amelia slept so peacefully in our king sized bed. Weeks of staying on the couch were affecting her sleep and making her a cranky little slave. Maybe all she really wanted to do was sleep and dream and so we figured what better way to accommodate her than with a long morning in our master bedroom. She slept so soundly, so quietly...

Even when we managed to bring her arms up to the bedpost and tie her wrists tightly in place, she didn't wake up. She almost woke up when we tied her feed to the opposite end posts, but not quite. Wow, she was such a deep sleeper.

We thought it was funny that we had to actually poke her awake to begin her special day.

"Wake up, slave," I said tenderly, caressing her face.

"Hmm?" She looked around her, immediately noticing her nude body, as well as the restraints pulling her limbs her in four directions. We were also naked, and from the looks of our excited genitals, we were already starting the party.

"Oh my God..." she said quietly, looking

around in disbelief.

"Surprise!" I said happily. "Today, we're making everything up to you."

"What?"

"Yes, we're going to give you a very special gift in light of how well you have been learning."

"I haven't been learning anything. I'm just letting you have all sorts of perverted sex with my body."

Jack excitedly spoke as he neared her blinking face. "That's why we're going to introduce you, Amelia, to the wonderful gift of giving."

"What's great about giving is that there is never 'too much,'" I added.

"What do you think, sweetheart?" Jack asked her excitedly.

"All right," Amelia sighed in boredom. "Let's get this over with. I want to watch to watch my soap operas."

I shook her fists merrily like a schoolgirl as I crawled on top of Amelia's chest and then inched my way over to her face. I sat my wet snatch, already lubed with an edible soluble, on Amelia's mouth and positioned myself just right. Now whenever Amelia spoke, her vibrating wisdom would tickle Kitty's kitty.

Meanwhile, Jack spread her legs gently and then entered her slave pussy with his hard rock cock. He sat up on his knees and grabbed Amelia's hips so he could give her the full throttle.

We were both so thrilled, we started fucking our house slave right away, giving her the gift of giving. I sat on her face and writhed over her mouth and tongue making her taste my cunt. All I could hear were mumbling sounds coming from under my pussy. Whenever she spoke, she massaged my leaking snatch. Whenever she stuck her tongue out hoping for some air, she licked my clit perfectly.

"Oh Amelia," I sighed deeply, "Eat my pussy...eat it..."

I sped up the pace and gyrated my pussy all over my slave's face, giving her the honor of my sucking up my sloshy cunt.

"Ohh!" I cried out grabbing my slave's hair for balance. I glanced over at Jack to see his progress with Amelia's education.

I looked over at my beautiful wife and smiled, as we both lovingly trained our sex slave. She made Amelia eat her wet cunt, while I destroyed her tight little pussy with a hard pounding. Amelia's cunt was a tight squeeze at first, but once I made an entry point I found her steaming hot pussy lube in no time. She was such a good, rough fuck...my little girl I always knew the way I liked it. I was so proud of her pussy. It took a licking but kept on ticking!

"I heard Kitty's voice cracking and saw

her face bouncing increase in speed. She was close to coming and was moaning in pleasure.

"Oh shit, Jack. I think I'm going to cum!"

"Come all over her face, baby. Make sure she swallows all of your yummy cum up."

"Yeah!"

"She wants to clean your cunt dry with her tongue. That's what she told me."

"Oh yeah!"

I watched my wife pound Amelia's face as she bounced up and down, her cunt contracting and spewing forth wonderful pussy flavors. "Ohhhhh!" she screamed hard, feeling that cum all throughout her body.

My honey relaxed and wheezed softly, finding my eyes and smiling peaceful.

"What about you, baby?" she asked. "Are you going to cum?"

My cock was weakening, after a long streak of pummeling Amelia's ultra-tight snatch. "Yeah...where you want me to cum?"

"You can come anywhere you want, baby. On her face, on her tits, in her hair..."

I started to gasp, and lose my breathing

control as I watched my cock ream her pussy and her pubic hair shift back and forth from the intense rhythm.

"I want to come inside. Come inside of her pussy."

"Yeah, baby. Fuck her pussy deep. Let all that cum out," Kitty said with an encouraging simper.

"You hear that, slave? I'm going to make you pregnant. All that hot sperm is going to flow through you and give your ovaries a hard fucking!"

"Yeah! Come in her, Jack!"

"Awwww!" I screamed as leaned forward and unloaded my cum inside my unwelcomed but very cooperative houseguest.

I made sure every last shot of cum filled her up and waited for my dick to deflate before making the big exit. I wanted every last drop of spunk inside her pussy.

As soon as pulled out I heard a queef and saw a load of spunk drip out of her swelling pussy hole.

We all waited quietly as we regained our breath. Kitty lifted herself from Amelia's dripping face and crawled over to her side hugging her nude body and kissing her perky breasts. I crawled over to Amelia's other side and lay at her nipple, relaxed, and feeling totally de-stressed.

Amelia spit up and managed to speak, not yet allowed out of her restraints, but definitely having earned some good points for being an obedient slave.

"So...what are we doing this weekend?" she asked nonchalantly.

Her face was resigned but her eyes were satisfied. Maybe she felt as if she was finally contributing something. Or maybe she accepted it simply—her new life and her new duties as a sex slave resident to our humble apartment. However perverse, our poorly devised plan worked too well. Instead of driving her away, we appear to have implanted Amelia as a new, permanent member of our family. Every time playtime begins, we push her boundaries a little further and feel horrible about our deeds afterward. But we can't stop ourselves. And she is unwilling to walk away.

Amelia has always been notorious for her "tall tales." Funny thing is if she goes around telling the true story of what happened between us, I don't think anyone would believe her.

## 2 MY DIRTY LITTLE SECRET

Whenever you think that life is too quiet, that people are behaving and that things are going fine and dandy, just remember this: small town life is never what it appears to be. There is always a scandal brewing. Someone you know is always thinking very bad things. People are just dying to do something stupid and screw up their lives. All it takes is one opportunity.

Take Britney. Looking at Britney, a nineteen-year-old girl, blonde and docile, and ultimately precocious despite all of her low cut tops and short jeans, you might think she's headed down the right path. You would see her in church, and you probably have bumped into her before at the supermarket and exchanged friendly hellos. She has the eye of every young soldier in town, and the heart of her family and friends who love her so dearly.

But there's another side to Britney and it's something that not a lot of people know. She's not just a naughty girl headed down a dangerous road. She is already a walking disaster, so blithely treading across a minefield of controversy. Have you ever noticed the way she rubs her belly in public? You're not supposed to know this yet...but she's pregnant.

And you will never guess whose kid is growing in her belly. I know Jonathan's family doesn't know and that's the town's best secret. After all, what would people do if they found out the patriarch of the Jones family is fucking his friend's daughter?

Don't ask me how I know. I just hear things from around town. From what I understand, Jonathan's friend adopted the girl when she was twelve. For most of her upbringing, the friend treated the girl coldly, hardly acknowledging her existence. Britney's mother Tamara took care of her most of the time. But the moment Britney turned eighteen, everything started to change.

Britney's mother Jonathan's friend, tired of his drunken stupors, and told Britney to follow her back up north where she has kin. To her shock, Britney refused and said she wanted to live with Jonathan. She really never had a "father" and I don't see why Britney refuses to acknowledge that. Maybe she's in denial? Or maybe she's just so desperate for affection she'll do anything to keep a man's attention.

And when I say anything, I mean anything. What's really creepy is that as soon as this girl turned eighteen, she was the one who changed. She volunteered to give Jonathan sponge baths, full body massages and all sorts of other sicko things.

Everyone who knows this sordid secret blames Jonathan. And yes, you don't have to convince me that Jonathan's a nasty old pervert. Every woman in town has been propositioned by Jonathan.

But believe me, he wasn't the aggressor. She went after Jonathan.

As soon as Britney began to grow breasts, she could sense how the men around her were affected. And yet despite having her choice of any guy in town—oh believe me the boys lined up for her phone number—the only man she ever seemed interested in impressing was Jonathan Jones.

To his credit, Jonathan didn't start having sex with Britney until she was eighteen—probably because he was conniving enough not to do anything blatantly illegal. Wouldn't you know, just a few months after she was legal, she was pregnant.

The really crazy part of it is that Jonathan's family refuses to see the truth. They always go around town calling Brittany a slut, and claiming she is going to hell just because she is having a baby out of wedlock. It's become the big town joke that everyone but the Jones' knows who Britney's baby belongs to. I only know Britney as a casual acquaintance, but even I know that the only man she ever looks at in worship, passion, and trust is Jonathan Jones.

What really infuriates me and most of the good townsfolk around here is the fact that Jonathan never stands up for Britney.

"That girl is such a little hussy," his mother said in front of me and a few other mutual friends. "I can't believe she has the audacity to flaunt herself and her bulging belly in public. She admits she's a whore."

"Whoever that tomcat is, he has a lot of explaining to do," Jonathan said with a laugh.

It's easy to see why Jonathan has such a powerful effect on Brittany. He has a strong face and a strong body. He's in his mid-forties and has a resilient face and very alarming eyes. His hair is thick, dirty brown, and curly. Jonathan has the ability to stare down anyone in his path. He talks loud. He thinks loud and obvious. And he doesn't care what people think about him—except of course for his dumb, unsuspecting family. And that dominant behavior is why Britney finds him irresistible. Dear, sweet Britney. Always looking for that father figure in your life.

I wished that she could have found someone strong, someone that could offer up that fatherly guidance she was sorely lacking. But not him. Not this perversion of nature. From what I hear around town, and it's practically unbearable to be around them, given their strange, sadomasochistic relationship they insist on flaunting in front of us.

Jonathan and Britney ate burgers at the local joint, cautiously keeping apart from the crowd, soaking in the sneers. It was socially acceptable for them to be seen together, only because Britney insisted she was spending quality time with "me".

"Jonathan?" she asked quizzically, in that cloying bimbo voice, leaning forward and giving him a close view of her supple breasts, busting out of that tight and sleeveless pink t-shirt.

"What is it, Britney?"

"I don't feel too good. Do you think you can get me some medicine?"

"What's wrong with ya?"

"I feel like gagging."

"There ain't nothing wrong with ya."

"Oh come on, Jonathan. Please help me feel better."

"Maybe you should stop eating all of this fast food bullshit and you'd feel better."

She pouted, leaning back and making the "duck face."

Meanwhile her boyfriend, Jonathan chomped his burger down.

"Your arms are so big...and thick," Britney said in a raspy voice. "Have you been working out?"

"I don't need to work out. I have a job," he grunted in responses.

She reached over and touched his bulging biceps, feeling the veins and the tight muscles. "So big," she giggled. "My Jonathan."

"I'm your boyfriend," he said in warning. "Don't be acting like a child, now."

"Why? I want to call you my Big Jonanthan. That's what you are. I may be adopted but I have never thought of you as my dad. The only real man I've ever known."

"I said, don't you call me that," Jonathan warned. "It's disrespectful."

"What should I call you then?"

"Call me sir."

"Sir, so formal! How about I just call you Big Jonathan?"

Jonathan rolled his eyes and kept

eating.

"You are not my dad, Jonathan. And I'm so proud to have a boyfriend like you."

She grabbed his hand and held it, alarming Jonathan and sending him into a retreat stance. No matter his badass attitude, he had to be concerned about how Britney was carrying on in the public eye. There is just a certain respectable demeanor fathers and daughters keep with one another. And Britney's fawning eyes were well beyond respectful. Come to think of it, so was the way she sucked on sundae cherries, all the while staring into Jonathan's eyes as if to suggest something shameful.

Jonathan leered back at her, roaring back in authority, and no doubt thinking of what he was going to do to her behind closed doors.

"Oh fuck me, Big Jonathan!" Britney screamed as Jonathan jostled her blouse and tore her breasts out from behind their shield. They went home and soiled the sheets just minutes after that shameful burger joint display.

Without the door even closing, Jonathan went straight for her breasts and bit her nipples, just to hear her little squeal.

He slapped her jugs hard as they made love, and every time he smacked them Britney lit up. "Punish me...punish me..." she groaned.

"You keep quiet, girl," he warned.

He shoved her to the bed, sending her into a free fall, breasts first into the soft sheets below. "Are you going to spank me?"

"Have you disobeyed me?"

"No."

"Yes, yes you have."

"When? What did I do?"

He reached under her pelvis to unbutton her tight jeans. As he pulled them off down past her ankles, he saw Britney's waiting backside, arching up and anticipating Jonathan's loving discipline.

"Is it going to hurt, Jonathan?"

"It hurts me more than it hurts you."

He swatted his hard hand across Britney's butt and waited to hear her squeamish response.

"Oh Jonathan, it hurts! It hurts!"

He spanked her again, this time a rapid succession of slaps. Britney's cheeks turned red the more Jonathan disciplined her.

"Why do you have to spank my ass?"

"Because I don't tolerate lying in this family," he said, roughly grabbing her head and turning it back to hear his reproof. "You don't tell the truth, you get punished."

"But I didn't do anything, Jonathan—"

He spanked her again, a hard five times in a row.

"Ohhh-!" she screamed, sucking on her own fingers.

"Don't talk back. You just take what I give you."

"You keep spanking me like that...you're going to make me cry."

"You going to cry like a little baby?"

"Mmm..." she pouted.

"Big girls don't cry," she scolded. "You going to be a little brat all your life?"

He smacked her on the cheeks again. "Hold it back," he demanded.

She bit her lip and stifled a scream.

"Hold it back!"

She struggled to maintain silence, even while Jonathan smacked her harder with each blow.

"You going to cry?"

She shook her head.

"Good. Now get up."

"I want you to put your hand through my pants. And reach in there and find something for me."

"Like what?"

"It will feel soft on the outside but very hard on the inside.

She followed his orders, clueless unzipping his pants and digging inside. When she pulled out his erect penis, she looked startled and scandalized.

"Oh Jonathan, what am I going to do with this big thing?"

"Stroke it. Like you're scrubbing the sink."

"Like this?" she asked, roughly stroking his throbbing member, not even bothering to lubricate it, since as anyone could guess, Jonathan liked it rough.

"Yeah," he groaned. "Now put it in your mouth."

"Eeeew!" Britney exclaimed in mock surprise. Why would I want to do that?"

"Are you questioning me?"

"No…"

"Do you want to get spanked again?"

"No," she sniffled.

"Then put this thing in your mouth."

Britney looked head on at the head and hesitated, playing into Jonathan's roleplaying.

"What are you waiting for? Don't you trust me?"

"Yes. I do."

"This kiss it. With your lips."

Britney did as she was told and stuffed Jonathan's penis into her mouth, looking up and begging for her father figure's approval.

I heard all the juicy details from a friend. But trust me, I really didn't ask for them. I mean some stories are just better left to the imagination, you know.

But my sources tell me Britney gave the best head you can imagine.

The thought of that pure, innocent little girl sucking that big bully's bulging penis...why it's just nasty.

Things only got worse in the months following. By the time most everyone—except Jonathan's dumb ass family—knew that Jonathan had impregnated friend's daughter, she was showing obvious signs of her with-child status. She had a big old belly and her breasts were already looking twice their normal size. Rumors started to spread that Jonathan was telling Britney to take hormones or something, but I don't really believe that.

You have to understand that some rumors are just rumors. Some people are so shocked at the reality of a situation they just have to invent all sorts of half-truths and urban legends to make the story a little more interesting.

Well, I can assure you the next sordid chapter is true because old Jonathan told me himself. He enjoyed bragging to his friends that he was having sex with Britney and took great delight in sharing filthy details. That's the only reason I know some of these things.

"Jonathan, I don't want to do this,"

Britney said, wearing a chic and modern maternity dress that still allowed her to have her big belly and look like a really classy lady.

"Princess, you don't have a choice. Now you know the drill whenever Jonathan gets horny."

"Jonathan, stop saying those words."

"Then maybe you should do as you're told."

"All you have to do is pull the shoulder straps off and lower your dress down."

She sighed, "Okay, fine."

"Because you're a big girl now and you have to take care of my needs."

"I know."

Now pull the dress down, Britney. That's a good girl," he said, watching her pull the straps and bring the top down past her chest.

She looked up in pouting resentment, but arched her back just so Jonathan could get see her big breasts and red nipples from an excellent angle.

"That's a good girl. Now head over to the couch. Because I want to suck on your titties."

"Ugh, do we have to do, Jonathan?"

"Britney, we've been through this. In order to prepare your big tits for breast-feeding we have to start pumping them in advance. Now sit back and hold your tits out for me."

"Okay," she sighed. She held her breasts firmly and made sure her nipples were hard enough for Jonathan to suck.

I know the truth of what happened because Jonathan told me. By all evolutionary logic, she shouldn't have been producing any breast milk before the baby was born. Then I found out the dirty secret. Jonathan had been prepping her by sucking her nipples four hours a day for months on end. He claimed he was doing it for the baby, so that it wouldn't be malnourished. But the bastard later told me he just enjoyed sucking Britney's fat titties. I believe he used that language too.

"Squirt me, baby," he commanded, crawling on the couch and setting his lips on her breasts.

Britney eyed him with a naughty gaze and squirted some breast milk right into his face.

"Yeah. Ohh that's a good squirt. Do it again."

She squirted more breast milk out, but Jonathan wasn't content to just suckle her like an infant. The man was obsessed with defiling this so-called virgin—though to be honest, she hadn't been a virgin for ages. Not after Jonathan was done with her.

He even took his penis out and rubbed his erection all over her squirting nipples.

When it was time to bang the girl, he

insisted upon her straddling him on the couch, only because the sick bastard wanted to see her big belly bouncing up and down. He told me the whole story, and bragged to me about how much wetter her pussy was when she was with child.

"Oh Jonathan! Fuck me, Jonathan!" she screamed riding him on the couch and bouncing her pregnant belly for his viewing pleasure. When she came, he sucked out her titty milk hard, because he wanted to feel that female ejaculation from two angles, you see.

It was a disturbing sight...actually, I don't even want to visualize it anymore. Because I just have too much love for poor Britney. And it kind of offends me to think of her in that way.

Now here's where the story gets really complicated. Jonathan may have been the only man who ever had Britney's attention, but he wasn't the only man who loved her so intensely. Justin, a young soldier on deployment, had always loved Britney since they were both twelve years old. But you see, he had that problem of being a friend first and a lover second. Britney never really had eyes for him, not while she was single and self-loathing.

However, things started to change when

Britney became pregnant. Her hormones were out of whack and she was spouting off on everyone—even her beloved "father figure" Jonathan.

"Sometimes you're an asshole, Jonathan!" she would scream to him in public. This not only infuriated Jonathan because of his perceived humiliation—it also upset him that she continued to call him Jonathan. It was a pretty twisted dynamic. He wanted to be her boyfriend, but seemed to hate it when she called him that.

"Don't you ever talk to me that way in public!" he roared. The scene was awkward as hell for us, but always ended the same way. Britney running off in tears and Jonathan shrugging off her "drama."

Well, one unfortunate day, she ran into Justin who was, well, his usual charming self.

"Hi Britney," he said cutely, as in love with her now as he had ever been.

"Hi Justin," she said coyly, still feeling his attraction, and wondering how a boy could ever find her attractive in her present state.

"You look beautiful. As always," he said with sincerity in his heart.

"Really? You really think so?"

And so it would go on. He would flatter her and she would deny his statements, buttering him up for more.

Of course, she would never really "give" him anything since she was with Jonathan and pregnant, and so figured the site of her naked writhing ball-like body would turn Justin off. But she was definitely paying attention to him—much to Jonathan's outrage.

"Are you fucking that young guy?" he asked her in a rage.

"No, I am not fucking him!" she said, standing her ground. "But we did share a kiss."

"You kissed him?" he asked in terror, as if kissing were the most intimate and humiliating perversion of all.

"Yeah. What can I say? He's a romantic. Like you used to be."

"Like I used to be?" Jonathan laughed, well aware that his harsh manner and rough language is what attracted Britney in the first place. I know old Jonathan is a hard ass for sure, but I know deep down he was terrified of losing Britney.

Britney had a decision to make, and it wasn't an easy decision, not a simple question of choosing the cutest guy or the best-looking suitor. She had to consider her future, her changing attitudes, and who would be a steady provider for her future child.

She also scratched poor Justin's heart a few times, telling him that she couldn't be with him—ever—not in the past, not in the present or the future.

Justin was ready to believe her, until the silly girl called him on the phone a few hours later crying her eyes out, and saying how much she loved him.

I tell you, it was a big sordid mess.

The one thing that was imminent is that Britney had to make a decision. And once Justin and Jonathan became aware that they were each other's worst enemies they both decided to settle the matter with a confrontation.

"You don't even love her!" Justin screamed to his new nemesis.

"I loved her longer than you. You just don't know how to treat women. And that explains why you're still a twenty year old virgin, boy."

"She told me she loves me. Because I'm kind to her, not like you. You're just her 'keeper.' Besides, everyone in town knows that your relationship with Britney is wrong. We all know it. And guess what? I'm going to take her away from you and make it right," Justin proudly asserted.

Jonathan thought about beating the hell out of Justin who was physically half the man big old Jonathan was—but I happened to be there that day they ran into each other, and talked Big John out of doing something stupid.

Instead, he was determined to win Britney back the old-fashioned way.

"I'm going to talk to her, Craig," he told me on the drive home. "Maybe I'm not as charming as little Justin. But I'm going to win her heart. You'll see. Everyone will see. We're going to be together."

"Well, do whatever you got to do," I told Jonathan, not really wanting to choose sides in this scenario.

"I know I have a hard way about me," he said regretfully. "But that's what attracted Britney to me in the first place. It's all I know, Craig," he said, a bit desperately, which was quite the change.

As I predicted, Jonathan and Justin had the same idea. And as bad timing would have it, they both journeyed to Britney's house that night, the two of them eager to make a proposal and sweep Britney off her feet. I sat on the sidelines, providing moral support to everyone, since I was not only the town gossip, but also everybody's friend.

Britney came to the door wearing a pink t-shirt and short denim shorts. Justin was dressed nicely, wearing suit pants and a collared shirt. Jonathan wore his usual casualwear, figuring he'd rather be comfortable when speaking his heart.

I was just wearing a jacket and a pair of jeans myself, so I tried to fade in the background as much as possible so that both fellows could make their point.

Justin started first. "Britney you know I love you. I have always loved you. Ever since we were just kids, I knew I was destined to marry you. You're as beautiful then as you are now. And I don't care whether you're with child or how many guys you've slept with. You will always be innocent with me. So come away with me and let's start over."

It was a nice speech, and Britney seemed genuinely touched. I figured it would be hard to compete with a speech like that, so it doesn't entirely surprise me that Jonathan chose a different angle.

"Britney, you are my lover." Justin looked at Jonathan in shock. "Sure, you're my girlfriend and not my real kin. But I always treated you like one of my own. Everyone in town knows about us. Even my own family has found out the truth. And they accept it. Now, girl, it's time for you to stop living like a child. All this stuff you're pulling is childish. You know it. It's time for you to get serious about raising that baby and acting like a mature woman. I'm the one who can best provide for you."

Justin's jaw dropped.

"After all, I'm Big Jon. And no one takes care of you better than I do. You and I deserve each other. We need to own up to that."

"What the hell kind of speech is that?" Justin shrieked in disbelief.

"He's right," Britney corrected suitor number two. "Jonathan and I are meant to be together. I don't know why I keep fighting it."

"Because it's insane!"

"Now, now," Jonathan interrupted, happy as can be. "I know how you feel. And Britney knows how you feel. I think the main lesson here today is that actions have consequences. Britney, your actions have hurt a lot of people. Do you see that now?"

"Yes, I do, Jonathan."

Justin looked confused.

"Now sex is one thing. But love is something precious, something that should never be taken for granted. Now, Britney, I know you're a young and passionate woman. And you have dark desires in you to share your pussy with a lot of different men. And I'm all right with that...so as long as you show me the proper respect."

"Oh, Jonathan...I do respect you."

"No, no. What you need is a lesson in respect. And a lesson to the men you have hurt. Now you have been very inhospitable to us all. And for that...you should be punished."

Britney looked at her Jonathan in

surrender and then looked to Justin. "You're right. I have."

"Now I want you to go over to Justin. And I want you to take your shirt off. And you should him how sorry you are."

Justin was confused beyond belief, but was so in love with Britney, it wasn't as if he could resist whatever was happening here. He was powerless to say no to her. Even if that meant a major compromise.

"Take off your shirt and show young Justin here your big milky titties."

She walked over to Justin and did as commanded, staring into his eyes as she dropped down her big tits and waited for Justin to make a move. I had never seen a young man so overwhelmed. All he could think of to do was reach out touch those melons finally sampling what had been denied to him for so many years.

"Craig," Jonathan yelled to me. "Go inside and get a picnic blanket so we can lay on something comfortable. We're going to have an old fashioned outdoor fucking today."

Did he say "we"?

Britney was already off the porch and giving Justin a lusty French kiss by the time I went inside the house. I wasn't sure what I would see when I came out, but sure as hell wasn't about to miss it for the world.

When I went back outside, I saw

Jonathan standing over Britney and Justin who were laying on the picnic table. Justin was lying back and Britney was sucking his little frightened cock like a sex-starved hussy. Justin was stunned and was yelping every time Britney stroke-sucked him, wetting his dick with her slobbering mouth.

Just as the boy thought he had enough, Britney one-upped him and gave him another wet surprise. She squirted his cock with her tit milk just so she could get in a tight titty fuck.

"Ohhh!" Justin blurted out with a wide opened mouth, seeing more of his true love than he ever thought possible. Britney stuffed that cock back in her mouth and tasted her own milk, all the while staring at Justin in that dreamy, schoolgirl crush sort of way. Yeah, this was something she wanted for a long time...and old Jonathan was very kind to give her a lifelong fantasy.

But the girl's discipline wasn't finished. Jonathan had further plans for his wayward child. "You're not done by a longshot, girl. You hurt a lot of people here today. And you have to be punished for everything you did."

"Yes, Jonathan."

"Craig, get your ass over here."

"What? Me?" I gulped nervously.

"Yeah, you, you dumb son of a bitch! I

know you're the town gossip. And I know how you're always looking at my daughter with lust in your eyes."

Britney turned to me and stared.

"Well, stop being a pussy. Come over here and take what you want. My girl's a slut today. Because sluts should be treated like sluts. Ain't that right, princess?"

"Yes, Jonathan. I'm a slut," she said with a smile and a kiss blown my direction.

I hesitated for a moment, but hell, when was an opportunity like this going to come around again? I suppose I did have a little bit of a crush on Britney, but I was about the age of Jonathan and never thought much of the opportunity. Until, that is, Jonathan's little debutante fuck party.

Britney got up so she could lower her loose meat sandwich onto Justin, who was writhing and shivering, trying to hold his cum back.

When I approached, she looked at me from behind and situated her big ass just so I could appreciate it.

"You want to fuck my pregnant daughter's ass, Craig?"

"Well...I don't know how to answer that, Jonathan."

"Just shut up and fill that hole."

I obliged. Britney stared at me in wonder while I unbuckled my jeans and let them drop to the floor. A beautiful young woman I had hardly ever talked to, and now suddenly, I was given the rare treat of penetrating her most intimate part.

She turned away from me and bent over on Justin, giving him more milk squirting action, while giving me ample room to see and touch her tight little asshole.

I put my hands on her ass and enjoyed the internal vibrations of her moaning. I licked my finger before sticking it in her, giving her at least a little lube for the tight squeeze ahead.

"Ohhh Jonathan...he's sticking it in my ass."

"That's right. That's what happens to bad girls, honey. Are you sorry for what you did?"

"Oh..." she sighed, "Yeah..."

My dick was aching hard by now as I watched Britney's gyrating asshole tempt me, dancing about and begging me for an insertion. I bent over and grabbed my cock by the hard shaft. I popped it in her warm hairy hole, gently at first.

Britney made delighted little squeals, acknowledging my shy cock.

"Oh Craig...I never knew you liked me that way."

I grunted and groaned as I gradually increased the speed of my thrusting. "Oh Britney..." I couldn't help but grab and fondle her big tummy from behind, fucking this mommy to be in such vulgar fashion.

"Yeah?"

"Your asshole is so tight..."

"Thank you!" she said in a throaty voice, enjoying a double pounding in both of her holes.

"Oh Craig..." she whimpered. "You were my first..."

"What?" I asked in a gasp, coming very close to losing my load.

"You were the first man to ever fuck my ass. Thank you for being...so gentle!"

Her voice cracked and she let loose a loud scream.

"Don't stop!" she said grabbing her tits and spraying Justin in the face yet again. Keep...fucking me!"

Jonathan walked over to her jumpy little face and unzipped himself, flopping out his cock. "As your last punishment, you're going to take this into your mouth. This is what we call Quiet Time. Understand?"

"Oh Jonathan...three cocks in me at once?"

"That's right. So maybe next time you'll think before you speak."

"Ohhhh God!" she suspired.

Jonathan shoved his big dick in her small mouth and face fucked her harder than either of us. Maybe because he was the one who really loved her. In any event, she gagged him down hard and I almost felt sorry for her.

Until I remembered, Oh that's right...she likes it that way. That's her dirty little secret.

Britney sucked and fucked us for almost an hour in broad daylight and on her front lawn. We fucked vigorously, all over a carefully placed picnic blanket.

Thankfully, when you live in a small rural town you are given a measure of privacy and distance. No one saw us or heard us, and I suppose that story became one of the many urban legends floating around town.

When we were ready to cum, Jonathan made sure it was a team effort.

"Gentleman, we're all going to cum in this bratty child at the same time. Hold yourself and wait till my count on three. One...two...three!"'

It was beautiful, like an orchestra of sperm exploding at the same time, filling up every hole of this woman's young, fertile body.

She unleashed a tidal wave of an orgasm, squirting all over Justin's cock and his face, and spasming hard for me, rocking my sputtering dick into oblivion.

Yes, Jonathan occasionally did lend Britney out to strangers and friends...but only when she was a bad girl.

I tell you, life is never that quiet. Things are always happening. And sometimes all it takes is one opportunity to ride a beautiful pregnant woman in the end.

# 3 PANDORA'S BOX: KINKY LATINA STYLE

The first time you move out on your own is always an exhilarating experience. Having just turned twenty, I was ready to take the plunge. Of course, having only a part-time job, I could barely afford standard rent. The only reason the landlord George was considering giving me a place was because he knew my parents. If he so much as looked at my credit or asked for an application with income levels, I would probably be stuck living at home with mommy and daddy for another five years.

Fortunately, George was on my side, and so was Lupe, the assistant manager to the "La Casa" apartment complex. The first time George gave me the keys to go look at the apartment, I was in seventh heaven. A castle of my own!

Oh sure, it was small and the paint and carpeting was pretty shoddy. And I blame the maintenance guy for that, not to mention Lupe who figured if little boy Scott was getting the apartment, it sure wasn't worth a full shampoo job.

I loved the silence, the eerie tone of nothing taking place. While I love mom and dad, there's just something magical about a boy's first apartment. And yes, I was living only a short distance away from my parents, but what mattered was the "buffer zone" it enabled me.

I looked at the bedroom. All I needed was a mattress and a sheet, and I could finally invite a girl back to my place and lose my virginity. Call me old-fashioned, but I figured I wasn't ready to have sex until I could actually leave my room and have my own transportation.

Of course, the décor was rather depressing in there. Maybe I should have invested some money in furniture and decorations before I become the master seducer. I know that the key to attraction is confidence. But man, it's hard to stay confident when you have to face your parents every day and ask for favors.

My moving out was a great first step.

The next day, I approached the front office, expecting to see the stone-faced

George but hoping to run into Lupe. Of course, I was only going to talk business with Lupe since she was the one who signed contracts in George's absence. But really, what horny boy wouldn't want another chance to talk to a 40-year-old Latina MILF?

Lupe was exotically beautiful, having huge natural breasts, which she tried to tuck away behind a blouse and sweater, and a tight body kept in shape from an active lifestyle. That mean old George still had her scrubbing carpets and cleaning apartments whenever paperwork wasn't waiting. Oh yes, she had a great body and I couldn't help but stare at her tits through her T-shirt and her bubbly ass through her one-size-too-small jeans. She was not only sexy in the typical way but also truly an international specimen. She had dark red hair and slightly arrogant eyes. But the most charming thing about her was Lupe's "loopy" behavior. She was known as a bit of an airhead and talked in that adorable Latina bimbo sort of way. Maybe all the women resented her and the authority in her voice when she had to convey a message, but all the guys loved Lupe.

I didn't really know what Lupe thought of me because number one, I was just a scrawny kid who was living with his parents. Though I must add, a lot of girls do describe me as cute. And not cute in the Justin Bieber sort of way. More like a young Lorenzo Lamas, if you remember that show. I remember it because for two years, there was nothing else on cable at 4 p.m. Number two, Lupe was forced to talk and be nice to everyone who entered the office, so who was to say if she was sincere about anything. All I really hoped was that she saw me as someone more than just another residential hopeful.

"Hey Scott!" Lupe said to me, as we both headed towards the office door, she coming out of a mommy minivan and myself emerging from an old 1991 Mercedes-Benz—the only car I could afford.

"I see you got a new car."

"Yeah, it's a Mercedes."

"No shit," she said coolly.

We both went inside and seated ourselves, directly across from each other, as she was getting to work and I was waiting patiently in the visitor's chair. "So I liked the apartment and paid the deposit. Is everything good to go?"

"Yeah," she said calmly, already taking care of some paperwork. "Just wait here a minute while I finalize your application."

"Cool."

I waited awkwardly, so unclear of what to say but oh so clear on what I wanted— her gorgeous body, her pouty lips all over me. I felt almost foolish bragging that I had my own place.

"I haven't exactly told my mother. And well...ummm...how do I say this?" I laughed nervously. "I'm thinking of moving a girl in with me. And my mother's not going to like that."

"No, she's not," Lupe said in that distracted but sanguine sort of way.

"Yeah...." Of course, there was no girl yet. But part of me was hoping Lupe would volunteer for the position. Or a few positions.

"But everybody's gotta' grow up," she said assertively. "So what do you do for work?"

"Hoping to get a job as a writer."

"Ohhhh, that's neat," Lupe said excitedly. "I'm going to school for teaching. And one of the things on my test is writing...how do you say...essays? Essays on books and authors and stuff like that. Maybe you could help me with it."

She didn't really ask, but I nodded surely, expecting my full cooperation. Then again, she didn't have to ask.... I would use any excuse to invite Lupe to my front door.

"Sure. How's your class going?"

"It's good. A lot of the guys, the young guys there, are freaking out because the work assignments are getting harder. I tell them, 'you can do this!' And they say, 'nooo, it's too hard!'" She laughed. "But I'm like, that's what it takes to make a career, you know? You gotta work hard for what you want."

"Yeah. You're right. When I studied in school, writing was my favorite subject."

I waited in silence again as Lupe concentrated on the application, crossing some T's and preparing my new residency. I couldn't think of anything else to say. When she finished the application, she had to wait for a few moments to process the data on the computer.

To my disappointment, instead of flirting with me, she just looked through the newspaper advertisements and killed a few minutes in time.

But I was more than willing to listen and play along.

"Wow, juice is on sale. You get two juices for one dollar. That's a good deal, huh, Scott?"

"Sure. But what I really want is to taste your juices, Lupe."

No, I didn't actually say that, and I only thought that statement hours later. But boy, that sure would have changed our relationship in a hurry.

That night, I slept in my new apartment. Having no mattress yet, I opted to just sleep on the empty floor. The thought that Lupe's bare feet may have been walking where I lay did help me to masturbate. Jesus Christ, I felt myself becoming one of those pathetic guys who drool over women but who run and hide as soon as they make eye contact. I felt it necessary to tell Lupe how I felt.

Of course, it's somewhat difficult to tell a woman with a son and a boyfriend that you sincerely want to have sex with her. I talked to her son a couple of times; he seemed affable, if a bit alarmed at my presence. I guess there's no polite way to introduce yourself to a kid and say "I want to boff your mom."

The one thing I had going for me was that Lupe was afraid of getting married and seemed totally unthreatened by me— not to mention the writing assignments she was receiving from school.

I pondered on the possibilities of how to approach her in a "new light," but within a matter of hours, I was back to my old creepy self, lurking around the Laundromat at 2 a.m. I always saw Lupe doing laundry in the weekday, so I figured I would spy around the quarters and see what I could find. For the first two visits, I found nothing.

However, by visit number three, I discovered something interesting. The maintenance room was unlocked. I opened the door and beheld a basket of female laundry. I knew it was female because I immediately noticed bras, panties, and a bootie sock. My imagination suggested that the clothing may have been Lupe's and she probably would have been loopy enough to forget to lock the door. I couldn't steal all of it...but surely, she wouldn't notice just one pair of panties missing, right?

The next evening, I received a knock on my door. To my joy, Lupe waited through the peephole. She was wearing her usual MILFalicious T-shirt, sweater, and jeans, never bothering to dress up for me. And why would she? She was gorgeous in absolutely anything.

"Hey Lupe!"

"Hi, Scott. I figured I'd drop by. You weren't sleeping, were you?"

"No, no. What's up?"

"Remember we talked about you reading over my essays? I just want to make sure they make sense. So I won't get an F."

"I'd like to give you an F," or so I thought to myself, still working on saying something cocky or at least kinky.

I reviewed her mini-essay and respectfully applauded, it being a few paragraphs of gibberish and juvenile observations.

"So what do you think? Not good? Not feelin' it? That's what the kids always say.

I ain't feelin' it."

"No, it's good. Let me just make some corrections...."

The more I read aloud, the more we both laughed at Lupe's bizarre misspellings and grammatical errors.

How can aged stupidity feel so sexy to a smart, young writer? That's the arrogance I need all right.... Now why can't I convert that into some flirty dialog?

Maybe I'm just not the flirty type. After all, my only line up to that point was...

"So how's the teaching profession going?"

"Pretty good. I like teaching. It's what I do to my boy all the time anyway."

"Yeah...so you're a teacher. I might have to give you an apple."

"Believe me, I need one."

It was an unexpected answer and I looked at her for a moment, wondering if that was a signal or just an intellectual belch.

"Well if you ever need one, I'll give you one."

Yes, it was lame...but I did manage to look right into her eyes and imply a lot more.

To my unnerving, the comment made her tensed up and she quickly fled from me, turning around and taking her paper.

"Scott, shame on you! You shouldn't be talking like that. Your mother and I are friends!"

"Umm...I don't know what you're talking about."

"You know what you said," she said with a haughty look.

"I didn't mean anything by it."

She shut the door behind her, leaving me to bask in my embarrassment.

A few seconds passed. To my surprise, she came back in, not even bothering to knock.

"Oh good, you came back. Listen, can we not mention this to my mother?"

"Or your girlfriend?"

"I don't have a...."

"Yeah sure, I don't believe you."

"I don't. I just say that to...you know, sound less pathetic."

Lupe shut the door behind her and walked closer to me. She went out of her way to avoid eye contact, perhaps not willing to fess up to what she was doing. She unzipped my pants, leaving me a quivering, sighing mess.

"What...what...." I figured maybe now is not the best time to ask why.

She put her hand in my pants, frantically searching for my dick, as if to hurry up and leave the scene of the crime. She found it buried underneath my shirt and underwear—unfortunately still briefs at that point.

I remember feeling her long pink nails

along my shaft, which she carefully kept clear of my prick hole. She gripped my cock with her first and proceeded to rub it back and forth, never once spitting and sucking. She wanted my skin to chafe. She didn't want to give me an explanation or an apology. She just wanted to jerk me off until I came.

Something was wrong with the scenario. She was giving me the porn fantasy I always wanted...but was not giving me a special moment. She was robbing me of something. Molesting me. Or in her insane words...

"Stay still! I want to yank it off."

"Uhhnnn...." I reached for her head but she backed away in warning. She continued stroking my aching cock and speaking gibberish. "Look at that little worm. So nasty. You're a nasty little boy."

"Uh huh...."

"Don't talk! Just let me pull that worm off."

I almost giggled at her strange attempt at dirty talk but remained silent so as not to kill the mood.

"I want to pull it off!" she said in frustration, as she increased the speed, yanking my cock skin back and forth without a care in the world as to how I was feeling. I didn't tell her to stop. The fact is I worshiped her enough to let her hurt me.

I may have been ready to cum, but she avoided getting any precum on her hands. The moment I ejaculated she sent all my cum to the carpet.

"Ahhh..." I sighed, still looking for eye contact but receiving not a look or a word.

Lupe left the house and didn't bother coming back for a few days.

Whenever I ran into her during daylight, she ignored me, probably feeling guilt—or even denial—over what she had done.

The next week, I decided maybe the secret to uncovering this sordid mystery of a relationship was rising to the challenge of her mind games. I waited until I caught her in her minivan, accompanied by her boyfriend and her toddler-aged son.

"Hey Lupe!" I said happily, putting her in distress.

"Hello, Scott," she said uncertainly. "Can I help you with something?"

"Well, I wanted to talk about what happened the other night."

She opened her eyes in terror and quickly got out of the van to meet me.

"Just a second," she said to her family.

"Yeah, the other night my sink flooded. I really need to get someone to look at it."

"Follow me," she ordered, escorting me to the office door, which was just a few feet away. We entered and she fumed. "Don't ever talk like that in front of my family!"

I said nothing. Instead, I reached out and grabbed her full bouncing breasts—molesting her back for a change. I felt it was equal punishment, a grab for a grab.

"What are you doing?" she screeched.

"I'm sorry. I just want to touch you...."

She glared at me in resentment and maybe even a little spark of interest. "You come to me tomorrow night. My apartment. You cross me again, you little pervert, and I will tell George to kick you out on your ass."

"Yes, ma'am."

She left the office and put on her best front.

I did arrive at her house the next day, dressed in what I figured was a cute but casual combination of black pants and a collar shirt. To my surprise, the house was quiet. No sign of kids or of a jealous boyfriend. I waited for about thirty minutes on the porch, wondering what the hell Lupe was thinking. A half hour late, she walked up to the patio, holding groceries and wearing another T-shirt–sweater–jeans combination. Her disinterested look warned me against bringing up her late arrival. Without a word, she unlocked and opened the door, allowing me inside.

"Go to my bedroom. Get undressed."

She went and put her groceries away, in no particular hurry to appease me. I stripped down to my underwear in record time and waited on the bed. The bed was mommy-like all right. Not really sexy, but time-conscious and fairly comfortable. It was a bed made for sleeping. Like she implied, maybe it had been a long time since anyone gave the teacher a big apple.

Lupe eventually made her way over to the bedroom, having taken off her sweater. She leaned on the doorway and took note of my body.

"You look so sexy...," I said.

"Don't say anything, Scott."

She walked over to the bed and pulled out some handcuffs. She showed them to me and finally made eye contact, as if to warn me and as if to remind me that it's too late to object. She pushed me down on my back and handcuffed my right wrist to the bedpost. She did the same to the other wrist and made sure I was stretched out far and immobilized.

She took her time, enjoying the sight of me squirming uncomfortably. She brought my feet out and foot-cuffed me to the opposite end, using the southern bedposts.

I tried to smile in encouragement, but couldn't help but feel threatened. She enjoyed the power trip and stared at me, again without words, for a few lingering moments.

The only problem was that she had forgotten to take off my underwear. And I was too flattened and stretched to move.

She had a very scary solution—she whipped out a pair of scissors. I remember thinking this is going to be very, very good or very, very bad.

She climbed atop the bed and approached me, dangling those scissors.

"You know this is wrong, Scott."

"Yes..." I muttered, equally terrified and turned on.

"You're a dirty, disgusting boy."

"Yes."

"What did you expect me to do? Strip naked and show you my agarraderas?"

"Uh huh...."

"You're a nasty little animal."

Lupe slapped my face, showing her teacher's authority. The longer I stayed silent, the kinder she became. She raised her arms and pulled off her T-shirt, showing me her 40 DD bra, which could barely contain her big mommy tits.

I sighed in trepidation.

She unhooked her bra from behind and slowly inched her way forward. She pulled her bra straps forward so that her bra would fall of naturally after a long, delayed wait. When her bare titties finally bounced in front of my face, I was stunned.

Everything I ever wanted and it was out of my grasp. The more I desired to kiss and suck on them, the farther back she would move. She enjoyed denying me the pleasure even more than she wanted to indulge.

But I accepted her discipline. Merely seeing her beautiful body in an unclothed state was the thrill of my short life thus far.

"You like that, muchacho? Amo guanabanas grandes!"

The only other titillating thing she could do at this point was to say something in Spanish. That did it. I was almost ready to cum.

She took the scissors and placed them near my crotch, looking at me in warning.

"Be careful," I said helplessly.

She cut my underwear through with the scissors, bringing my hard cock out. My mother's worst nightmare had happened: I ruined my underpants. But I guess Lupe and I were even.

"Sacate el pene," she said, crawling over to my dick and putting her cold hands on it.

"Yes...whatever you just said, yes..."

"Say, 'Chupe leche del pene.'"

She almost smiled as she played with my hard cock, feeling its veins and bulging head.

"It's what a man says to a sexy woman.

It means 'Suck the milk of my cock.'"

I nodded in complicity, as she left my eyes behind and focused her attention on my lonely dick. This time she made sure to get it wet. She licked the head with her lips tenderly for the first few seconds, only to spit on it in contempt.

"Ahhh...," I sighed, already squeezing and holding back a quick cum.

"Yeahhh," she said in her funny bimbo voice, so expertly sucking the milk out of my cock.

"Oh, Jesus," I whined, feeling every suck and lick like a burning fire. She didn't just blow me...she was cock torturing me, grabbing and pulling down the shaft while she sucked the head relentlessly. She wanted me to ache, to beg for release.

Instead of licking anything so sweetly or tenderly, she boosted the aggression. Just as I came close to cumming, she suddenly slapped the head of my cock. Surprised, I looked on and whimpered. "Owww...."

She squinted in aggression and slapped the head again before returning to a firm suck. Lupe wasn't much for licking. Maybe it was that strong-minded Latina spirit in her, but when she pleasured me, she took more than she gave. I was her cock prisoner, and to be honest, I didn't mind it one bit. It sure as hell wasn't boring or too corny. This was a first time worth remembering.

Anytime I came close to cumming, she would slap me again. The next time I exhaled, she slapped my balls, delicately balancing the pleasure and pain scale.

"Ohhh!" I cried out, not sure whether I was climaxing or yelling for her to stop.

"You're so nasty," she exclaimed, looking over my firm ball sack and pulling the unshaven hairs. "A woman doesn't want to lick your hairy cajones."

"Sorry."

"Little boy. You don't even deserve me," she barked. She eyed my nuts carefully as she squeezed the testicle skin, coming way too close to cracking a nut and paralyzing me. It all reduced me to a quivering mess of sensations.

"You want to feel my tetas?"

"Yes!"

"Do you?" Lupe teased me, putting her breasts ever so close to my raging hard-on but denying me the connection. "No. You don't deserve it."

She slapped the base of my shaft hard, not giving a damn how it felt for me, but loving it from her side of the bed. "Look at your little pito. You're not big like a man. You're a scared little boy. You can't fill me up, Scotty."

"I'm sorry...I wish I were bigger."

"All you are good for is to wipe my colita. You want me to use you? Use you like a tampon, you sick little boy?"

"Yes, Lupe...."

"Don't you ever say my name!" she warned, slapping my cockhead again.

"Sorry."

"Say, 'yes ma'am.'"

"Yes, ma'am."

"You want me to suck your little dick again? Maybe make it harder and longer?"

"Yes!"

"Yeah, I'm sure you do, little nasty boy."

She sucked my cock again, all the while tickling my balls with her long pink fingernails.

"You're not as big as my boyfriend," she reminded me. "His pito is much bigger. I hope you're smart, Scotty, because your dick is too small to please a woman."

"I know...." I shut my eyes and squeezed my pelvic muscles again, desperately trying to keep from cumming and ruining my amazing first date—maybe the only chance I would ever get to taste Lupe's spicy Mexican sweetbread.

"What's wrong? Are you cumming already? No, Scotty. You hold it in. Do you hear me?"

"Yes," I cried out, trying my best but already losing the war against my convulsing hips.

"Don't you cum! I didn't say you could cum. If you cum now, I'm going to leave you here!"

"No!"

"Yes! I'll let my boyfriend come home and find you and beat the shit out of you."

"No, please...."

"And I'll tell your parents too."

"No...."

"So don't you dare cum, Scotty. You hold it back. You hear?"

"Yes...I'm sorry...."

"You hear me?" She slapped my cock again and shoved it back in her mouth, sopping it up with spit.

"Oh God...you're making me cum...."

"Don't do it, Scotty," she warned nonchalantly, already planning my punishment.

"Ahhh...." I sighed deeply, already feeling my tortured cock spasming.

Lupe moved up slightly, just to put her massive tits in front of my ultrasensitive cock. Daring me not to cum, she began rubbing her big nipples against my cockhead.

"Ohhh ffffuck! Lupe! Oh fuuuuck!" I yelled as I started shooting cum all over her big tits.

She looked into my eyes, as I sputtered out shot after shot, leaving her gorgeous tits covered in my nasty cum. Her chest was left with a gooey mess and she seemed to resent me for my failure. As much as I wanted to make a soul connection by staring at her deeply, I just couldn't keep my eyes off her bouncing, cum-covered tits.

I panted hard, trying to catch my breath after the best cum shot of my life.

Lupe stayed in character—or who knows, maybe it wasn't a character—as she moved close to my face in dissatisfaction.

"I didn't say you could come, Scotty."

My own cum dripped onto my chest, falling from Lupe's skin.

"Now you're going to make it up to me."

"Whatever you want, ma'am. Anything."

"I'm going to treat you like you deserve it. Like a little nasty boy."

"Yes, ma'am."

"I'm going to use you to clean my pussy."

"Yes!"

"You like that?"

"Yes...."

"You sick little pervert. Does your mother know the kind of stuff you like?"

"No...please don't tell her."

"I might have to. Unless you do what I say."

"I'll do it."

"I'm going to sit on your face," she said as she unbuttoned and unzipped her tight jeans.

"Yes, please."

"I'm going to make you eat my smelly pussy."

"Yes, please...."

"I'm not even going to shower for you. I was hot and sweaty all day. But you're just going to eat me the way I am."

"I'll do anything."

"Because you're a little tampon," she said, pulling her jeans and red panties down while in a kneeling position.

"Yes."

"Just a piece of shit I clean myself with. You like that?" She wiggled her pant legs off and showed me her unkempt but very mom-like bush.

"Oh God, yes."

"Then you shut up and eat my pussy, Scott."

I mumbled excitedly in response as she sat up and moved forward, sitting her hairy pussy on my smiling face.

I mumbled something or another and Lupe seemed pleased by the pleasant vibrations.

"Oh yeah, Scott," she cooed, shifting her pelvis around and making sure my tongue went right into her wet snatch.

"You like that? You like how my pussy tastes?"

"Mmmm!" I screamed, but she responded with a little slap.

"Shut up and lick me, boy."

I did exactly what she said and licked her messy pussy all over my face. I licked her creamy snatch and dug my tongue up past her pubes and up to her big, swelling clit. I worshiped Lupe so much I swirled her own name in cursive all over her clit.

"Mmmm...yeah," she said, feeling the heat. "I like making myself cum. You're not doing anything, Scotty. You're just sitting there like a piece of Kleenex, waiting to catch all that mucus."

"Mmm-hmm," I managed to mumble.

"Ohh yeah," she groaned, squeezing her own nipples. "Oh Gaaaad...I love touching myself. You like watching me touching myself?"

I shook my head up and down.

"Don't move! Keep licking. I want to drown you in my juices, Scotty."

I did what she said, not bothering to breathe, only licking up and swallowing Lupe's drenched pussy.

"Ohhh!" she yelled, as she shook side to side, feeling her own orgasm building. "Oh yeah...faster...harder! Come on, Scott! Don't disappoint me!"

I doubled my efforts and ate her pussy so fast and hard I almost fainted.

"Oh Scott! Oh Scott! Yes! Drink my juices, Scotty! Drink my el jugo de coño!"

She opened her eyes wide and started shaking her entire body, ready to explode.

"Oh!!! I'm cumming on your face! Drink those juices, fuck it!

I opened my wet eyes, and all I could see as I gazed upwards was Lupe's dirty snatch, her cum-glazed tits, and her screaming face. It was enough to make me hard all over again.

"Oh Scotty! I'm gonna squirt! I'm squirting!"

She squirted a hard shot all over my face and made me drink up every last bit of her hot Latina juices.

After her wet and wild orgasm, Lupe gasped for a few long minutes, still sitting on my face without apology. She used my face to wipe her pussy juice clean and dry off.

When she finally crawled off of me, I took my own gasp of fresh air. It was nice to smell something besides Lupe's dirty snatch. But who was complaining? Certainly not me.

"So..."

Lupe headed for the shower, barely turning to me. "What?"

"What now?"

"Since my boyfriend is coming back in a few minutes, you better get out of here."

"Want to un-cuff me?"

"No, I don't," she teased, smiling wickedly as she left to shower. "You stole my panties, Scott. I knew it was you. Now you have to walk home without clothes on. That makes us even."

Gee, I thought to myself, I sure hope she's kidding.

She was. Lupe wasn't much of a writer,

a deep thinker, or even that great of a teacher, but she was an amazing mother fuck. She gave me the most creative, sexy, and outrageous first time a horny virgin could ever ask for. We never had sex again since she was taken and I was—as she accurately told me—just no match for her boyfriend. Still, I love the fact that she flirted with me long after our affair, even in front of my parents, which weirded them out big time. I know most people think "sweet" and "special" is what every smart, nice guy wants. The truth is even nice guys want bad girls, at least in the beginning. And the Pandora's Box I opened with one simple, inappropriate remark to an acquaintance was worth the risk.

# 4 A THREESOME OF HATRED

What is a man to do when two beautiful women love him? More importantly, what can he do when these two beautiful woman hate each other's guts? That was the predicament Pablo found himself in, as he courted two beautiful women, each one with her own financial and emotional baggage. Pablo was the savior, the good son and the nice guy, and felt compelled to care for them both—even though both girls despised the thought of sharing him with the other.

Of course, it was hard to fathom Pablo remaining faithful all year round to Aimee, his new American girlfriend, considering that he had already met and promised himself to Gunda, his German fiancée 12 months earlier. Then again, how could he possibly last seven months alone, in a cold and distant country, without feeling the warmth a good woman?

Both women assumed the most idealistic scenario: that Pablo would eventually leave one of them and settle down with the other, either in America or in Germany. Both women knew Pablo's love of Germany, and it was no coincidence that Aimee had German blood, with a touch of Irish. Gunda, on the other hand was pure German and could date her ancestors back to 1750, nine generations. Pablo was a dark-haired mutt, but a charming mutt, and knew how to sweet-talk a lonely woman, reciting the best works of Hesse, Nietzsche and Hegel, whenever his brawn, dashing eyes and debonair smile couldn't save him.

What was it about Pablo that attracted such high maintenance lovers? Gunda was in constant debt, and only really "wealthy" the few months that Pablo stayed with her in Thuringia. Whenever he went away to America to continue his schooling, Gunda would call him and demand that he wire money to save her from destitution.

Aimee was not poor but was plagued with medical conditions, and a touch of hypochondria, or Pablo figured, since she spent most of her week at the doctor's room and on the Internet looking up exotic diseases. Aimee had the money to do so, and would play Pablo's sugar mama whenever he came for a visit.

She let him stay in a Colorado cabin, while Gunda let him stay in her brother's unattended apartment. It was a double life of wealth and poverty, and yet the lucky bastard somehow figured out a way to achieve the upper hand in both relationships.

Not that his two lovers gave him a moment's rest.

"Are you still fornicating with that American woman?" thickly accented Gunda asked him in bed, raising her brow and aggression level. He smiled and took in her exotic beauty; golden hair, pouty lips, and a full but slightly tanned face. Like the classic German beauty, she had a thin figure but broad shoulders and a full chest.

"Aimee. My dear, why must you continue to be a master at guessing and keeping still? You know what the greats say...you must not want to see everything."

"I do not understand that," she said firmly. "All this question requires is a yes or a no. Are you still having sex with her?"

"I cannot forget that I know her. She is a part of my life."

"But I am your future!" she commanded him. "You cannot continue to see two women forever. What happens when we decide to move in together? She cannot live with us. You must let the other woman go. She does not love you like I love you."

"I'm trying to think of a way out of it, Gunda. You know I love you the most. You know I love Germany the most. If I could stay here with you, and leave everything behind in America, you know I would. But I have to finish my studies. For us. For our future."

"But there is nothing of good to come from raising the hopes of a foolish American girl."

"She's not a girl. She is 35, just like you."

"Do you only date women the same age? Two years younger than you are?"

"For my entire life, I have only made love to two women. Many men from America go through two women a day for their entire lives. All I am asking, my love, is just for a little more time."

He kissed her tenderly.

"You may only have two coins of small value, Mein Herr. But don't make a fool of yourself thinking you can save them forever."

Gunda hated Aimee and made no mistake about it. Whenever she discovered a picture frame of Aimee in a suitcase, or an old love letter in a file, she fumed.

"Another picture of your American whore!" Gunda screamed, as Pablo unpacked his suitcases back for summer vacation.

"I'm sorry. I forgot to take it down."

"You keep pictures of your mistress around the house. It is humiliating!"

"Around the house? In my suitcase! I have a right to my own possessions, Gunda."

"Keep all the photos you want," she said with a grimace. "Soon, you will have to be a man and choose. And I know you do not love her. She is not pure German. She is a handicapped mick with tainted blood in her veins."

"I will deal with her in my own time."

Gunda continued to rave about her competition, only to break down within minutes and make a friendly request.

"My sweet, sweet man," she said with a glowing face. Your lieschen needs to borrow five hundred dollars."

"Again?"

"I have financial needs! The only other option is to prostitute myself in the streets. Is this acceptable to you?"

"Fine, fine," Pablo said, as always, caving to pressure.

When he arrived home in America, the

story was similar but with a different face.

Aimee stood before him, folding her arms, as he lay down his heavy suitcases.

"You're late," she hissed.

Aimee's angry face still couldn't invalidate her gorgeous features. Her hair was Irish red and her skin slightly pasty. She was not as thin as Gunda, but had a marvelously voluptuous figure that inspired her lover. Her eyes were starry and her eyebrows were moderately heavy, giving her a distinctively Irish-German flavor.

"You are so beautiful, Aimee," Pablo remarked. "Even when you scourge me."

"I thought you said you were breaking up with her. With her! Your slutty German friend! I don't understand why you can't just stop seeing her!"

"I have known Gunda for many years, my love. Before you, she was the only woman I had ever loved. I can't just toss her out like an old newspaper."

"Well!" Aimee barked in response. "How are we ever going to get serious about marriage if you're carrying on with other women?"

"Just give me time, my angel. Just give me time."

He held her head tenderly and looked into her eyes, asking for absolution. It was always seemed to work, because they were such soulful little windows into a much gentler, artistic world.

"I brought you a present."

"Oh?"

"I was visiting Amsterdam. And I picked up some bon-bons, lollipops and pasta shells for you."

"Why would I...ohhh!" Aimee said with an excited smile.

Aimee may have had all the money but Pablo had the overseas connections and the brilliant way of sneaking sweet treats pass airline attendants. He was also her agent on the inside, since Aimee was far too shy to ever take advantage of her Colorado residency and ask the unthinkable to her already irritable doctor.

"Oh my God..." Aimee sighed, spacing out and for once, dropping all of her medical pretenses and aches and pains. "I love you Pablo! I'm so sorry I ever doubted you."

Pablo laughed softly. "My only crime is that I love too much."

"I know," Aimee said dizzily, gripping on to Pablo's arm and caressing it mindlessly. "Maybe in another world...Gunda and I could have been friends."

Pablo looked down at her and shrugged it off, figuring Aimee was talking goofy and ready to pass out as usual.

He enjoyed her when she was quiet and calmed. Whenever he took his treats away, the nagging side, the "American

Woman" would come out and demand his full attention. He figured, at least he knew what it took to calm Aimee's constant stress. Indeed, without him, much of her life would be nonexistent. She might as well be a hermit without his guidance, his confident direction, and of course, his overseas stress relief remedies.

One might even say, she needed him.
Pablo intensified his study efforts and spent two months apart from both women, though he made it a point to call them and give reassurances of his unending love. When he finally finished his studies for the year, he sent both women a scandalous message.

I HAVE CHOSEN YOU. LET'S CELEBRATE. MEET ME AT THIS ADDRESS. I WANT TO HAVE OUR HONEYMOON IN CALGARY.

Both women were ecstatic, though confused as to why he insisted upon them meeting him at the Calgary Marriott Downtown Hotel in room 619. Both women went through great trouble to arrange a flight and taxicab to the hotel, though of course, Pablo insisted upon paying their way.

Aimee fixed herself up nice in her prettiest black scalloped boudoir lace dress, figure flattering and a sophisticated but sexy v-line. She even wore the dark makeup, the one she figured made her look whorish, but which Pablo loved. Gunda attended the celebration too, wearing a chic one shoulder-striped dress with multidirectional stripes and a mid-thigh hem. Gunda arrived before said time and entered an empty room. She made herself at home and sat on the comfy recliner, sipping champagne.

The hotel was quiet and decorated with red curtains and red roses, a wonderfully romantic night had been planned.

Aimee arrived fashionably late and entered the same hotel room. "Pablo?" she asked.

Gunda sat up and looked on in shock. "You!"

"You!" Aimee screamed after a long pause. "Oh my God! He didn't..."

"You! Why are you here? You are not supposed to be here."

"Why am I here? Why are you here? Pablo wrote me and told me to meet him here. He said he chose me. You lose! Bye-bye!"

"No! I have the letter in my hand. He clearly stated that he chose me."

Both women furiously reached for the letter in their respective purses. To their disappointment and disgust, sure enough, they imagined they read their name, when in fact the entire letter actually said was "YOU."

"I cannot believe he would do this.

Again," Gunda sighed, falling down on the recliner.

"I can't believe it either! You've poisoned his mind!" Aimee snarled. "He told me he loved me. You were nothing but a booty call to him."

"A what?"

"A boo...just forget it! Pablo is mine and I think you better leave!"

"I am not going anywhere," Gunda screamed.

"Well neither am I! I'm going to sit down right here and wait so that Pablo can ask you to leave himself!"

"You will be the one surprised, American girl," Gunda muttered.

"So you think, Nazi whore. By the way, Pablo told me what you said. Pure German, give me a break."

"You doubt my blood? You are not even a real German! You are a European, American mutt!" Gunda snapped back, smacking the couch arm, and inching farther and farther away from her threatening acquaintance.

"Believe me, if I didn't feel sorry for you—knowing Pablo is fixing to break your heart—I would punch you in the face," Aimee warned.

"You?" Gunda laughed. "Stupid American girl. All you know is talk. You have never fought or lived in the streets."

"Like you have? The only reason you're

not on the streets is because Pablo supports you!"

"And he doesn't support you?"

"No! I have money!" Aimee said with a snarky head bob. "I'm the only taking care of Pablo."

"Oh I see. Taking care," Gunda laughed. "Meaning he buys you drugs. He keeps you sedated."

She squinted in disdain. "You know, I'm finished talking to you! Just shut up! I'm telling Pablo today. You're out of his life forever."

"We shall see, little girl."

Pablo took his sweet time, shopping at the mall and buying his favorite cologne and brandy combination. By now, both women were waiting for him, possibly fighting, or perhaps trading stories and making peace.

Not likely, he figured. At least, not yet.

Pablo entered the hotel room with beaming confidence. Even when he saw two resentful faces glaring back at him, he kept his vivacious smile.

"My love."

"Who the hell are you talking to?" Aimee yelled.

"You invited us both here?" Gunda screamed.

"Ladies, please. Relax. Don't ruin my good mood. I brought champagne, and very lovely cologne that I want to you both to smell."

"Are you crazy?" Aimee demanded. You can't keep doing this, Pablo. You have to choose between one of us."

"Yes," Gunda added. "And I know you will choose wisely."

"Yes, yes he will choose wisely!" Aimee snapped back and then turned to Pablo. "Make a decision! Now! One of us is staying and one of us is being wheeled out of here on a stretcher."

Pablo sighed as he sat his bags of mall presents down. "My loves, I have chosen. Next year, I graduate. I am going to work here, in Calgary. There is a wonderful career ahead of me. And I wouldn't even consider moving unless my two lieschens came with me. I want you both. I want to love you both."

Both women laughed at the audacity of his request.

"Who do you think you are?" Aimee bellowed in disbelief.

"Jung had a wife and a mistress. Henry and June Miller shared their bed with Anaïs Nin. Why is it that we all have to be so conventional? You are both the most beautiful women I've ever laid my eyes on. I had none before you, and I shall have none after you."

Aimee and Gunda both got up, ready to storm out, balking at Pablo's request and his nonchalant attitude.

"Well, I am not going to be part of some weird, German threesome," Aimee spited. "I am a one woman man."

"No, I will not agree to a threesome. Not with this ugly woman."

"Excuse me? Look who's talking! Your skin looks like carpet!"

"Your skin looks like a vampire!"

"Ladies, please! Stop the bickering."

Aimee walked towards the door. "I don't have to take this. I'm going out so that you can tell this filthy German whore goodbye once and for all. And if you don't call me back, I'm going to keep on walking.

"No, you won't."

Aimee and Gunda both looked at me in surprise.

"You both need me. Just as I need the two of you. We complete each other. Gunda, my love, I take care of you and will continue to take care of you. I make sure you have enough money to live comfortably. With my new job and easy hours, we'll have so much time for fun, for hobbies and relaxing."

He turned to Aimee, wearing the same jubilant face and spoke his love with his hands, heart and entire soul. "And Aimee, my dear Aimee. The woman who captured my heart and wouldn't permit me to suffer another night alone. I have so much of my soul invested in you. I couldn't leave you if I tried."

The girls bickered again and repeated their threats. Pablo, however, had another point to make.

"And every relationship is based on giving and taking. What I have to give, no other man is going to give you." His smile was sincere but with a hint of ego, as he couldn't help but brag about his tangible assets. "Gunda, no other man is going to take care of you. Not with you spending $5,500 a month on restaurant bills. And the only reason your brother is letting you stay in his house is because I pay him behind your back. Do you really want to try to life in Germany on your own, with no friends and no capital? Poverty is not fun, my dear Gunda."

Gunda listened in sullenness.

"And Aimee, my beautiful American princess. You have no strong man in your life. Not only am I going to give you love, but I am also providing you with guidance. I am willing to fight the world for you, just so you can live in total comfort. And there is the other matter…"

Aimee listened, already feeling crabby and shaky, from not having her fix. "I suppose you do have the strength to walk away from me. But in doing so, you would also be walking away from my many treats, sweets and presents. You know the ones…the ones that make you feel good, relaxed and at peace with yourself."

"My loves, I have sacrificed a great deal to make you both very happy. And I am tired of being taken for granted. If you love me back, then you will accept this arrangement. You could walk away now...but you're not going to. Because I like taking care of the both of you. We're a family. I don't want to break apart our family."

Pablo walked over the bedroom, strutting confidently, having made a hard point to argue. "Now then, I have money to give and brownies to pass out. But before I do, I need to know you accept our new family arrangement."

Both women looked at each other in contempt, but feeling powerless to actually resist Pablo's will. After all, a life without Pablo was a life of responsibility, a lonely life, and a life so different from the one they had built and become accustomed to.

"Now then. Let's go into the bedroom and make this official."

Pablo disappeared into the bedroom, leaving both women confused, staring at each other, and slightly horrified.

Pablo plopped himself down on the bed and waited for his loves to enter and lay beside him. "Maybe I didn't make myself clear," he pronounced loudly. "If you don't come here and do this, I will leave the two of you. And you will never see me again."

Aimee and Gunda sighed, entering the bedroom and folding their arms in nervousness.

"I don't understand...what are we doing?"

"We're kissing and making up."

Aimee and Gunda awkwardly sat on the edge of the bed, awaiting Pablo's orders.

"I feel your hatred, your detesting of each other. From here on out, I demand that you resolve these feelings of anger and jealousy in the bedroom. Because I will not fill my mansion with bickering, drama and violence."

Pablo unbuttoned his gray shirt, preparing for a wild night of reconciliation. Now then, "Who goes first? Shall I make love to Gunda while Aimee watches? Or shall I make love to Aimee while Gunda watches?"

The two women remained silent, looking at each other, and back to Pablo, not really having an answer. Pablo began to speak...

But suddenly, Gunda objected. "I am not a second place. If your American whore wants to watch us fuck then let her."

"Wait, no!" Aimee interrupted. I am first. I am the one he really loves!"

"Then I guess..." Pablo said putting his arms on both of his loves' shoulders, "We are going to make love together."

Pablo unbuttoned and unzipped his pants. As he slid the pants down, all could see that he preferred neither boxers nor briefs. He had nothing to hide and instantly exposed his hard cock to his two mistresses.

"Kiss each other. Kiss each other over my cock."

Aimee and Gunda reluctantly moved towards his center, despising the idea, but despising the idea of losing his favor even more. As they kissed over his bulging head, they made sure not to lose the advantage—each angry woman fought for her half of Pablo's manhood.

Pablo relaxed and exhaled deeply, relieved to see his two lovers cooperating for a greater good. They both sucked and licked his cock sweetly, wetly, and smudged it up with sexy red lipstick.

He directed both women's gobbling lips downward so that they could taste his smooth balls. Aimee licked his right nut while Gunda licked his left. When Aimee felt ambitious and swallowed one, Gunda reacted quickly and returned the favor. Pablo groaned happily, enjoying the sight of his angry lovers touching cheeks and grazing each other's lips.

"Take your clothes off. Both of you. I

want you to see how beautiful the both of you really are."

Gunda and Aimee glowered at each other, and did as commanded. They hardly even looked at Pablo, but stared tightly at each other, wondering what the other thought of the intense competition. Gunda easily slid her one strap dress off and pulled it down to her feet, and off the bed. She let Pablo admire her green bra and thong, which complemented her tight ass and firm stomach.

Aimee took things slower and raised her blouse over her head, letting her provider admire her bubbly tummy. Next, she slid off her skirt and showed her two new spouses her black underwear. She was the modest one; a bit shy, but very accommodating and willing to please to her most trusted companions.

Pablo waited patiently, desiring to see the four breasts he loved the most.

Both women unfastened their bras quickly, and tossed them to the flower, letting their breasts bounce freely. He signaled for them to come closer, to smother their fleshy pillows in his face.

They both waited on their knees as Pablo turned his head to each, sampling Gunda's pink nipples and Aimee's violet nipples.

"Touch your breasts together," he ordered. "What's mine is hers, and what's yours is hers too."

Aimee and Gunda did as commanded, and held their breasts up, pushing the areolas together—a gesture of unity.

"Now take your panties off. I want to see your pussies."

Gunda beat Aimee to it, and slid her thong off quickly. She crawled to the other end of the bed just so she could spread her legs wide and show her snatch proudly. Aimee took more time, the sensitive type, and only obliged after gentle caressing encouragement from Pablo. She slowly slid her panties down, showing everyone a neatly trimmed red bush.

"Gunda, my love. Aimee has taken a great risk here. Show your appreciation. Taste her. Put her in your mouth."

The two women eyed each other in mistrust, but Gunda followed through with the request, so eager to prove herself the dominant wife. She crawled over to Aimee's shivering pussy and spread her lips apart roughly.

"Uh!" Aimee cried out.

"It's okay," Pablo assured her. "It's going to feel good."

Gunda found Aimee's clitoris and licked it. She didn't merely lick it like a lollipop—she tongue slapped it and sucked it with fervor. While she may have thought she was injuring her competition, it was actually Aimee's favorite maneuver—the same one Pablo used when he gave her head.

"Ummm!" Aimee screamed with her mouth shut, trying to stifle a most reluctant pang.

Gunda was ruthless and attacked Aimee's clit without mercy. She sped her tongue like a helicopter and slowed down only to suck it dry.

"Oh!" Aimee said aloud, dripping across Gunda's face. "Oh Pablo...hold me."

"I will, I will."

Pablo grabbed onto to Aimee's waist and held her firmly; assuring her it was okay to orgasm at the lips of a woman. Gunda sucked that clit hard, missing Pablo's taste; he put his hand on the back of her head, assuring her too that she was performing well.

"Ohhhhh!" Aimee loudly grunted, shoving her pussy upwards and mashing into Gunda's face. Gunda spit out Aimee's pubes and continued tasting her snatch.

"Make her come, Gunda. Make her come."

"Mmmm...Ohhh...Pablo! Pablo! I think I'm coming..."

"It's okay!" he said with a gentle squeeze. "Gunda wants to make you happy. Just let it happen. Let it out."

"Ahhhh..." Aimee said, gritting her teeth and letting herself orgasm.

"How did that feel?"

"Good..." Aimee cooed.

"How did she taste?"

"Sweet," Gunda said, moving away from Aimee's dripping pussy.

"Now lie down on your backs, the both of you," Pablo commanded. "Since Gunda has been waiting to come, I am going to fuck her first. Aimee, be kind to your spouse. Play with her breasts. Love her nipples.

Pablo crawled on top of Gunda and filled her aching snatch with his hard cock. It was a tight and dry squeeze at first, but that's just how Gunda liked it. He shifted inside of her, waiting for a good stroke. When he found it, he sped up the pace and fucked her vigorously. Pablo leaned up on his knees as he continued fucking her, giving Aimee adequate room to assume her role.

Aimee leaned over on her side and touched Gunda's bouncing breasts. She squeezed nipple, making it hard and easy to suck on. She had never kissed a woman before, much less made love to her. So her opening kisses were shy, a bit reserved. But they only helped to bring Gunda to orgasm quickly. Aimee licked one nipple and squeezed the other in rhythm, complementing Pablo's steady stabbing.

"Ahuuhhh!" Gunda screamed, coming

powerfully and experiencing a full body quiver.

"Ahh!" Pablo exclaimed feeling the heat. He withdrew from Gunda's wet pussy and walked on his knees over to Aimee's face. "Suck my cock. Taste Gunda's pussy. See how sweet it is."

Aimee hesitated a moment but then agreed, unable to resist Pablo's assured poise. She sucked Gunda's pussy off his cock, drying it up for another wet encounter. When he withdrew, he wiggled his way over to Aimee's waiting pussy and filled it with fire.

"Ohhh...Pablo..."

"Can you feel it...your vaginal creams mixing up. The three of us are becoming one."

Pablo thrust his cock into Aimee's wet pussy and unleashed his base desire, pounding her pussy like a toy.

"Ohhh God!"

"You like that?"

"Yessss!" she screamed, her G-spot throbbing and approaching orgasm.

Gunda became impatient and crawled over to Pablo's shaking butt cheeks. She put her hands on them and then kissed them tenderly. She massaged his firming balls, challenging his staying power, and grazed his anus with her meandering fingers.

"Oh Pablo! I'm coming again!" Aimee

screamed, swatting the bed on both sides.

Pablo shifted himself to the center of the bed and signaled for Gunda to climb atop his waist and ride his wet, Aimee-drenched cock. She sat herself down willingly, mixing creams with her rival and straddling the life out of chaffing dick.

"Fuck!" Pablo yelled out, the sight of Gunda's big tits bouncing taking its toll on his senses. "Aimee..." he cried out in panting passion, "I want to taste you. Your precious fluids. Sit on my face."

Aimee sat up to take her position, but was interrupted again by Pablo. "Face Gunda. I want you to both to look at each as the three of us come together."

The redheaded one obliged and sat her pussy carefully across Pablo's face, letting his tongue invade her precious privates. Gunda and Aimee stared at each other as the passion intensified and their bodies pulsated, shaking from orgasmic imminence.

This time, their faces were not full of hate. Rather, they looked to each other as lost siblings, perhaps even feeling a newfound respect.

They had so much in common after this encounter. They shared genital fluids, shared Pablo's cock and even discovered their similarity in orgasms. After knowing someone so intimately, how could they ever go back to being mere enemies? They were a special sort of acquaintance; it was a ménage à trois of competing family members.

Pablo was close to coming but was giving it his all in the last few moments of breath. He was fucking Gunda with all his might and losing the battle to contain his explosion. He was also tongue-lashing Aimee and sucking her snatch juice into his mouth. He was ready to implode, having brought together the two loves of his life.

Both women were approaching a second orgasm, and as they felt the rage building, they looked to one another. They both leaned in close so that they could share a kiss together—in the midst of orgasm and with Pablo's cock scent aftertaste.

Pablo tried to scream as he ejaculated powerfully into Gunda's slippery snatch but was covered in Aimee's gluey goodness. Aimee and Gunda screamed for him, reaching a simultaneous orgasm and hugging each other tightly.

It took a long minute to settle things down, their voices still panting and the bed soiled with cum and sweat.

To celebrate their newly found threesome affair, the group took a shower together and experimented with mutual bathing. Pablo was so proud of what had happened; the two most important women in his life embracing each other, and soaking each other's tits in soap. The water washed them all clean, and wiped away the hate.

The animosity and mistrust was certainly palpable, and by no means erased. And the two competitors never stopped their staring contest. The only difference was that now, whenever they fought, whenever they thought ill thoughts, they could literally taste each other's pussy—still fresh in mind from that glorious one night.

The three lay in bed later that night, and fondled each other's intimacy, finding comfort from the cold Calgary breeze from a nearby open window. They both caressed Pablo's penis, he being placed in the middle. But Aimee's hand eventually did rub Gunda's elbow, and Gunda did lock fingers with her former foe.

"I love you," Pablo said.

"Love you, Pablo," both women chimed in.

"Goodnight, Gunda."

"Goodnight, Aimee."

It would take time, yes. But the beginnings of something beautiful had already been set.

"Life doesn't get any better than this," Pablo said. "Eating, drinking, and making love. All for today. Nothing great in the world has ever been accomplished without passion."

## 5 HOW MANY MEN DOES IT TAKE TO SCREW A WIFE?

"Hey honey. Wake up. Honeeeey, wake up."

"Mmm."

"Come on, don't be a sleepy head all day. We have big plans today."

"What?"

"Don't you remember? You don't? Tee hee! Come on, silly. Today's the day. You know the day. We talked about it, remember?"

"No..."

"You said I could have anything I wanted. Well, I decided. Your birthday girl decided. And I know what I want."

"What?"

"Well, here's the thing. I don't want just 'one thing'. I want everything. I want it

all. And you're going to give it to me.
You know why?"

"Why?"

"Because you want to make me happy."

"Uh…"

"Yes, yes, you do. Don't pretend that
you're falling back asleep. I want you to be
awake while this happens. Honey, I just
have to tell you the truth. Our sex life is
running on empty."

"What?"

"You can't do it for me. You never give
me orgasms. Your cock is too small. You're
impotent most of the time. I am a woman
with needs. I am 33 years old and nearing
the sexual peak of my life. I can't just sit
here and age with you. Do you
understand?"

"What are you saying?"

"I'm saying that for my birthday, I am
going to have sex with whoever I want.
And you can't stop me."

"What?"

"That's right. I'm going to have sex with
anybody and everybody. Whatever cock I
can find on short notice. Friends,
coworkers, acquaintances. Maybe even
random people I meet on the Internet. This
is a day all about me. And you're not going
to say a word."

"I don't think so…"

"No, you're going to keep quiet. You're
not going to object over my selection.

You're not going to complain or whine or do any sniveling. Be a man...or have you forgotten how to do that?"

"I just...I...I don't know."

"Don't worry. I'll make it easy on you. All you have to do is just sit back and watch. That's kind of what you do anyway. You watch TV. You watch me take my clothes off. You watch porn. So all this is for you is more watching. Watch me, honey. I want you to just sit back and relax today. While I have my fun. Okay?"

"Gee honey, I don't know."

"Now, now. You have your fun, I have my fun. If you get through the day and be a good boy, I will let you have a special reward. Okay?"

"Reward?"

"Yes. But only if you last the entire day. If you give up or pussy out like you usually do, then no reward at all for you."

"What's the reward?"

"You don't get to know until later. But I assure you, it's a good one. You will be so happy you cooperated. So do we have a deal?"

"Hmm..."

"Honey...you don't have a choice here. You are going to watch this happen one way or another. Do you understand?"

"I guess so."

"That's right. Now, the big question is, who am I going to have sex with today?

Hmmm...let's see. Let me get out my rolodex. Or hell, I'll get out your rolodex. This is on a first come, first served basis. Because my womanly parts are aching, baby."

"Well maybe I can...you know...maybe I can help..."

"What? What are you talking about? Stop babbling. Now just sit back and relax, baby. Because wifey needs to make a few phone calls."

"Well...I guess."

"Hmm. The question is, who should I call first? Let's see. Who do you not like? I know you hate John, the neighbor from across the street. You're always complaining about him. Why do you hate him so much anyway?"

"Well..."

"Oh I know. Because he's handsome. Because he's a musician. He's got that rock star personality that women find irresistible. The truth is, I find him irresistible too. I think I want him, baby."

"No..."

"Yes. Yes, I think I do. I know John's always too busy for you, to help you out. But something tells me he would help your wife out in a heartbeat. So I'm going to just give him a call. Okay. Now you be quiet, okay?"

Hey John? Hi, this is Krystal. You know, your next-door neighbor? Yeah hubby's off working overtime today. You know how that goes. Well, not so much you, since you're wealthy and my guy's sort of a bum. Hahah! But anyway, I was wondering if you could come over later tonight. Why? Well, there's a problem with the sink. The pipes need cleaning. And I know that you're a jack-of-all-trades, being a househusband and all. I'm not supposed to tell you this, but well, my baby gets so jealous of you. He has to work so hard every day and you get to just have fun, play your music, and explore your creative gifts. Hahahah! Yes, you can imagine how much he complains about you. So anyway, I need my pipes cleaned. And I need the carpet scrubbed. So do you get what I'm talking about? Okay, I think we understand each other. You're a man of many skills, I know. Tell your wife Melissa I said hi. So I'll expect to see you around seven p.m. Great! See you soon, John.

"Well that was fun. John seems really excited."

"No. I—I don't really want him over here."

"Well, we already made plans, honey. You know what? I think he actually knows that I'm just inviting him over for sex. That must be why he was so eager to come, since he never really wants to hang out with you."

"Y-You're going to have sex with him?"

"Yeah. I must admit, I find him very attractive. I like sex with rock stars. Does that make you jealous, baby?"

"Yes.

"Not really much attracted to accountant types. Like you, baby. But don't worry...I still love you. You work hard to make sure we have very average things."

"Well, I try my best..."

"But your best is so limp, sometimes. Ah, but honey? I still believe I have an open schedule today."

"Oh no."

"Hmm. Who else could I call? Is there anyone you can think of that might be able to satisfy me? You know, give me a big orgasm for a change?"

"No...no one."

"Oh! You know that black guy from the pawnshop? The one that's always staring at me? The one who makes you jealous all the time?"

"No, please, please not him."

"Yeah, I think we have a winner! What do you say, let's give him a call. Now honey, just be quiet, okay? I don't want you to ruin my date tonight."

Hello, this is Krystal. Is there a black man working there? There is? Great!

"Sorry, honey. I don't remember his name. But then again, it's not really important, you know?"

Hi there. This is Krystal. I think we've met a few times. I know you're always, ahem, staring at me when we're in your store? Hahahah, no problem. No need to feel embarrassed. Look, I'm having a party today. Would you like to come over? Well, the thing of it is, it's invitation only. And the guest list is very short. Yes? Really?

"Oh honey! I'm so excited. He said yes!"

"But...but..."

"Be quiet, honey."

Great, I'll see you around nine o'clock then. Four, one, one, two Blanca Boulevard. Bye-bye, ya big mandingo.

"No. This is not good."

"Wow, I don't know about you, honey, but I'm really getting kind of hot just thinking about all this fun. But...I still want some more."

"No. Please, no more."

"Let's see. Who else is there? Hmm, I can't really think of anyone else we know. Oh, I know what I can do. Yeah, you can tell by my big smile that I have a wicked idea, right? How about I go to that GregsList website and post an ad, giving my home address?"

"No. I don't think that's a good idea..."

"Why not? Are you really worried or are you just jealous? Honeeeey?"

"What?"

"I think you're failing the test."

"No, I'm not."

"I told you before; I want to have sex with a stranger today. Why does that bother you? Sometimes, the best sexual relationships are the ones we create with strangers."

"But..."

"I suppose you'll never know about that, huh? Because you've already promised to be faithful haven't you?"

"Yes."

"Well, that and you have no balls and you could probably never ever find a woman to sleep with. I mean, you got to be really charismatic and handsome to do that! Like John."

"I wouldn't do that."

"I know you wouldn't honey. Well, I think I'm going to post an ad, honey. So you wait right here while I type it up. But I'm going to let you read the ad, okay?"

"No, I don't want..."

"Great. Just wait there. I'll show it to you."

Hi everyone. I'm alone tonight. My cuckold husband likes to watch. He will NOT be participating. Only watching you and what you choose to do to me. No rules. Just make me happy. I'm a housewife about 30 or so. I have big boobs. I have an average waist, a few extra pounds, but all in the right curvy places. Brown hair. I sometimes wear glasses but sometimes wear contacts. About you: I'm not picky tonight. Just show up and be real. This is not a fake ad. My phone number is 555-431-KRYS. Call for the address, or email me and you can surprise me in person.

"What do you think, honey?"

"I don't like it...it's just..."

"What? Oh, you're just jealous. Why are you so threatened? You should be happy that all these guys are going to satisfy me. That means less work for you."

"But...I like pleasing you."

"Oh, stop it. You don't even know what a clitoris is, do you?"

"No."

"Well, don't worry. Maybe one of the guys will be nice enough to show you. How about that?"

"No, really, no..."

"We'll see."

"Well, I'm going to take a bath. I want to smell nice for the guys coming over later today."

"But...you never bathe for me."

"Hahahah! No, silly, of course not. Just wait here for me. Hey, and if any of our guests come over early, just let them in for me, okay?"

"Oh honey look! Someone already

answered my ad!"

"Oh no…"

*My name's Jerry. I have a couple of friends hanging out tonight. We're definitely real. We just want to come and taste your pussy. Do you have a picture you can send us?*

"Oh, I guess I better be nice to them. I don't want to chase the boys off."

"Boys? But they're so young…"

"But honey, young boys have staying power. Plus, they can get hard really fast, even after they ejaculate the first time."

"Tell you what, I'm going to go out for some condoms, just in case someone doesn't want to ride me bareback. I want you to stay here and choose a kinky picture to send the boys, okay?"

"No, I can't do that…I don't think…"

"Honey, are you acting up again? If you don't help me with this, you get no reward."

"Ohhh…all right, I guess."

"Good boy. I'll be back soon."

"Hello?" Krystal asked into the phone, then turning to her husband and said, "I think I better put him on speakerphone."

"Who is he?" her husband asked.

"Someone from the Internet I think."

"Oh no…"

"Is this wifey?" the man on the other line asked.

"Yes. You read my ad?"

"Do not talk. I am your master. I will be coming to your house at midnight. Do not ask questions. Do not say no to me. If you pass the test, I will make you a very happy slave." Krystal heard the man on the phone speak.

"Okay," she replied.

"Good. I want you to shave your pussy before I get there."

"I can do that, sir."

"From here on out I am your master."

"I understand, Master."

Krystal hung up the phone and turned to her husband.

"Wow! Can you believe that, honey? This guy is serious. And so authoritative. I really like it when guys take charge like that. I wish you could be that sort of strong man...but it's okay. You're a good provider."

"But...I want to be strong."

"Shhhh, I've got to shave my pussy, baby. Okay? That's the way our new friend likes it."

Ring.

"Hello?" Krystal's husband asked.

"Hey honey. Sorry, I meant to leave you

a note," Krystal said.

"Where are you?"

"I'm at John's house. We had a change of plans. He asked me to come over here. He's very busy, you know."

"Then just come home."

"No, no, I want to be agreeable and nice to our neighbors. Anyway, I just wanted you to listen in."

"While what?"

"While I suck John's cock, baby. He's standing right here, ready to let me blow him."

"Hey there, neighbor!" John yelled into the phone.

"That's him. He says hi. Are you ready, baby? I didn't want you to miss out on this. It's going to be a good sloppy blowjob." Krystal purred to her husband on the phone.

"I don't want to hear this...," her husband said.

"Oh, stop it silly. Now you just sit back and listen closely okay? Mmm...he's pulling his pants down for me. He's wearing boxers, in case you're wondering. Wow, my heart is beating so fast! Hahahah! I'm so excited. Oh, wow. Honey, you wouldn't believe the size of John's penis. It's like literally twice the size of yours."

"Don't just sit there, suck it!" John demanded.

"Oh sorry! Okay, John wants me to get started, baby. But you can listen in, okay?"

There was silence from her husband.

"Mmmm...wow it's hard fitting my mouth around his cockhead. It's hard as a rock. Mmmm...oh yeah. You like that? Mmm-hmmm...shuuuuurrppp...Mmm. I love sucking your cock, John. Mmm. You know I never give my husband oral anymore. I don't know...he just doesn't turn me on. Not like this. Mmmmm...spuuhhhh! Oh yeah, you like me spitting on your cock, John? Is this what your wife does?"

"Oh yeah. You should come over sometime when she's here. She'll fix you up good," John said.

"I will. Mmmmmmmm. Honey, I'm licking his hard veiny cock right now. He's moaning, so I must be giving him good head. He tastes so good. He must eat healthy, because he tastes so much better than you. Mmmmm hhhffffpppphhhhh! Mmmm, I love the taste of his pre-cum. I'm licking it all up. I just want to gobble his cum, honey. What do you think of that?"

"Ugh. I don't like this," her husband responded.

"Why not? Honey, remember our deal? Don't ruin this for me. John has a beautiful cock. Mmmm. You want me to teabag his balls, honey?"

"No."

"I will. Aaaaah. Aaaaah. Oh yeah, I'm licking them up. They're salty. I can tell when this big boy comes it's going to be a big load. Where do you think he should cum honey?"

"Nowhere."

"You want me to swallow it?"

"No, anything but that."

"Oh yeah, hubby wants me to swallow your cum. Mmmm face-fuck me, baby. Gacccckkkkk...ahhcccckkkkk...mmmuua aah! Oh baby he's fucking my face so hard! Mmmmm! Uhhnnnn... Ahhhhh! Oh honey, he's close to cumming. He's going to cum in my mouth. I want to swallow him cum. You want to hear it baby?"

"No!"

"Ah...oh yeah swallow that cum, Krystal. Mmmm!" John moaned.

"Urggghhhhh. Gurrk. Mmm. Ahhhh! Oh yeah. I swallowed it, baby. He came in my mouth. So much spunk...I think I better go brush my teeth. I'll be home soon. Bye, baby."

"Baby, wake up. Sorry to interrupt you from your naptime. But someone's on the phone. I think he wants me to have phone sex with him," Krystal said, shaking her husband's arm to wake him up from his nap.

"Tell him no."

"Silly, I told you, I'm taking on all comers today. Now you just keep lying there. I'm going to lie down too. And I'm going to touch myself. His name's Kyle."

"No. I—I don't want you to..."

"Honey, stop being difficult."

Krystal turned her attention back to the phone and the awaiting Kyle and said, "Okay. I'm ready. Yeah my husband's right next to me. No, he doesn't look very happy—hahahahah! Hold on, I'm going to put you on speakerphone so hubby can hear you."

"Mmm...tell me what you're wearing baby," Kyle demanded from the other line.

"I'm wearing a nightie. A blue silver color," Krystal responded.

"Take out your nipples so your pathetic husband can see them."

"Oh yeah, you like that? You want me to pull my titties out?"

"Squeeze them. Imagine that I'm licking them."

"Oh yeah...I wish you were here right now."

"What's your husband doing?" Kyle asked.

"Looking kind of angry and jealous. I don't think he likes what we're doing."

"Too bad. If he were a real man, this

wouldn't be happening."

"I know. Are you touching yourself too?" Krystal asked the man on the phone.

"Yes. And I'm thinking of your big tits while I jerk myself off."

"Mmm yeah, I like that. What would you like to do to me?"

"Handcuff you to the bedpost."

"Ahhhh...yes. I like that idea. What else?"

"And eat your pussy out while that sack of shit watches me."

"Yes baby...yes! Mmmm, oh God, keep talking."

"Touch your clit. Rub it."

"Hey honey? You see this right here? This is my clit. This is the special spot a woman likes rubbed. My new boyfriend wants me to rub my clit."

"Your husband doesn't know what a clitoris is?"

"No. He never gives me an orgasm. Never."

"What an idiot."

"I know...ohhhh...I'm touching my pussy for you, Kyle."

"Describe what you're doing."

"Rubbing my clit back and forth...mmm...feeling myself becoming wet. And thinking about you. I wish you were here..."

"Me too. I would be eating your sweet, sweet pussy right now."

"Uh huh! Ohhh...you're already making me cum, Kyle."

"Cum for me, you slut. Make your pussy squirt."

"Oh my God! I'm cumming! Kyle! Ohhhh! Uhhhnnnn!"

"I have to hang up now."

Krystal hung up the phone and turned to her husband. "Oh baby, that was so good. Are you jealous?"

"No," he replied.

"Yes, you are! I can see it in your face! Funny honey. Well, I think I'm going to shower and get ready for my new friends. Aren't you having fun, baby?"

"I'm sorry, but this is the way it has to be, honey. I like when you watch me cum. But my new friend doesn't like our little arrangement. So I think it's best if you hide underneath the bed," Krystal told her husband.

"No, I don't want to do this."

"Honey, just do it. Okay? Don't make this any more difficult. Do not make a sound while he's here? Do you understand?"

"I...I don't I can promise that."

"If you don't, then no reward for you. Understand?"

"Oh...I guess so."

"Okay, now scoot. Get under that bed and wait. I don't want to hear a sound, not a peep from you. I've been waiting for a big black cock my whole life."

"That's disgusting."

"No, you're going to see disgusting soon enough. Don't worry honey, I'll try to describe what he's doing to me, so you don't feel left out," Krystal said, then left the bedroom to answer the knock at the front door.

"Hey there!" Krystal said to the large black man standing in her doorway.

"Well, hello sexy. So your husband not around?"

"Nope, he's out for the night."

"Well you are a very beautiful woman, Krystal. I've thought about doing this for years."

"Me too. Let's go to the bedroom. Whip it out. Show me how big you are. Oh my God. You're so huge!"

"Just for a pretty white lady like you."

"Oh my God. I don't even know if I can fit this thing in my mouth."

"Oh no, no. This big black stallion doesn't do oral. He wants your tight, white pussy."

"Oh gee golly. That's going to be a tight squeeze."

"That's the way I like it. Tearing up that gorgeous pussy."

"All right. Let's try this. Be gentle."

"I can't promise that."

"Did you bring a condom?" Krystal asked.

"No. I only do it bareback," the man answered.

"Good, because I want to feel every inch of that thing."

"Ohh...slide it in...oh yeah...deeper...OOOHHHH! Oh, fuck! Fuck! Oh my God you're so huge!"

"Oh yeah...take that cock. Take it all in nice and deep."

"God! Oh baby, you're going to fuck the shit out of me!"

"Mmmm yeah...I want to see your skinny white pussy gape."

"Oh fuck me with that big black cock!"

"Oh...pull it out. Let me look at it. Oh, my...you have to see this. His cock is so huge. I can barely fit him inside me..."

"Who are you talking to?"

"Nevermind. Keep plugging in there. Oh yeah slide it in and out like that...yeah."

"Now just hold on tight, because it's going to get fast and bumpy."

"Ohhh...yeah...do it fast...oh my God! It's so deep. Yeah...pound that pussy! You like fucking your white bitch? Huh? Is this what you were thinking about when you were staring at me?"

"Oh yeaahhhh!"

"Oh God! I want you to cum inside me!" Krystal exclaimed with a squeal.

"I'm gonna cum!"

"Oh yeah! Fill me up! Let it rip, fucker! Yeaaah!"

"Oh my God. His cum is dripping all over my gaping pussy. He's still trickling out cum. He just gave me a steam hot cream pie."

"Who the fuck are you talking to?" the black man asked.

"Hubby. He's underneath the bed," Krystal said.

"What? Let me see..."

The black man said shocked, "Damn it! This is some crazy shit. I'm out of here." He pulled up his pants and ran out of the house.

Krystal lifted up the bed skirt to look at her husband under the bed. "Peek-a-boo, honey! Oh baby, you should have seen it. I've never seen such a big cock before. I think my pussy is stretched out a bit. You want to see?" Krystal positioned herself on the bed with her legs wide open and pussy gaping while her husband crawled out from underneath the bed. "There. Look at it. Isn't it pretty?"

"The Master has arrived, honey. Please don't screw this up for me. The good news is that you get to watch this time. He wants you to watch. Just do what he says, okay?"

"I don't feel comfortable with that..."

"This is the last time I am going to tell you this! Stop being such a selfish asshole! It's my birthday!"

"Oh...okay."

"Hey there! Come on in. This is my husband. He's not allowed to speak."

"Good. I'm here to train your wife and make her obedient. Not to you. To me. Do you understand?"

Still silent, her husband nodded his agreement.

"Good. But during this time, I am going to talk to you. Your wife will follow my every command. She will not speak. You will not speak. As long as we are all in agreement, the training can begin." There was a pause and no one argued. Master continued, "Your wife is going to take her shirt off now, because I want to see her tits. I want to test them and make sure they are working properly. After all, they are just tools. Tools for my pleasure."

"Mmm..." Krystal moaned.

"Your wife's nipples are hard. I'm going to squeeze them now until it hurts."

"Ahhh!"

"Now I'm going to slap her tits around because it amuses me."

"Huhh...."

"How does that make you feel? Huh? This is just the beginning. By the time we're through, your wife is going to be in agony. I'm going to make her cum. Cum so hard that it hurts. Then, I'm going to cum inside of her. Your cum receptacle of a wife. And she'll be forced to have my baby. All because you're too much of a pussy to stop me. Look at her. She's masturbating already because she knows what I want."

"Uhhhh! Oh God it feels so good," said Krystal.

"What do you say, whore?"

"I want to have your baby...uhhhh...oh God...my pussy's so wet..."

"And now...HEY! Sit down! What do you think you're doing—" Master exclaimed when he saw Krystal's husband jump up.

"Now you listen to me, goddamit! I've had enough of this! I don't care who you are! I'm tired of everyone treating my wife like a slut! You get the hell out of my house! Go on, get before I kick your ass!"

"Hey! What are you doing? Wait! Don't go! Come back!" Krystal called after Master, then turned to her husband. "Honey, what the fuck? You chased off my master! Oh my God, I can't believe you ruined this for me!"

"I didn't like the way he was talking to you."

"I told you what would happen if you did this! Now, you get nothing."

"I'm sorry. I just lost my temper."

"It's too late to apologize now! You just

cost me what would probably have been the best orgasm of my life!"

"I'm sorry, dear."

"Just don't bother apologizing. Well guess what? If you thought the master was hard to sit through. Just wait till you see what's coming next."

"No...no...no more."

"No, nothing. You've already blown it. You get no love tonight. But that doesn't mean I'm not treating myself to some good sex for a change."

"Remember those boys I invited over? They're last on my guest list tonight. And however many of them come through that door, that's how many I'm going to fuck."

"No..."

"Yeah. And no matter what kind of whore they want, that's what they're going to get. And you can't stop them. There's too many of them. They'll kick your ass and take me by force, if they have to. So you might as well just sit back and let them fuck me however they want."

"Oh. All right. Fine. Just hurry it up. I feel depressed."

"You called this on yourself."

Krystal greeted the guys at the door with a bright smile. "Hello boys! Come on in. Don't mind him, that's just my loser husband. He's here to watch."

One of the boys responded, "Nice! Say you, loser husband. You want a blindfold or something? Because your wife is about to get fucked up."

"I...I think so. Because I don't want to watch."

"No problem! Jessie? Get old man Holmes here something to cover his eyes."

"But hubby wants to watch!" Krystal protested.

"You shut up, bitch!" one of the boys demanded.

"Sorry."

"Now you listen here, old man. I'm sparing you the sight of watching your old lady get reamed. But that doesn't mean you're getting off easy. Because I'm going to tell you what's happening. And if the more upset you get, the worst we're going to treat her. Understand? So if I were you, I'd just sit back and enjoy the story."

"Mmmm...oh honey...they're all getting naked for me. There's four of them. They're all pulling down their pants and whipping their hard young cocks out. I wish you could see this. It's so beautiful."

"You just hush up, doll face. I'll do the talking. Now the first thing we're going to do to your old hag is strip her clothes off. She has some big ass titties and we want each take turns titty fucking her."

"Mmmm...yeah stick it in between my

tits. Oh! Yeah!"

"Jimmy is going first. Oh yeah, he's got the biggest cock of the bunch. And he's going to stick that ten-inch rod between your wife's jugs. I want you to listen up closely to the bed creaking."

"Oh yeah, fuck my tits! Yeah! Put your young meat all over me..."

"But my other bud Sam is getting impatient. I think he wants to deflower your lovely wife's mouth. What do you say?"

"Mmmmmm!"

"Oh yeah. He's stuffing her mouth full of cock right now. Your hot wife is gobbling up that cock like a porn star."

"Mmmmpphhh!"

"Hah-Hah. Sam is stretching her mouth out though, making sure that little whore worships his cock right."

"Auughhhhh! Oh yeah, oh honey, I don't know if I can take any more of this. Ohhhh..."

"Now Alan's going to go and lick her bunghole. What do you think of that?"

"Oh shit! Eat my ass! Oh God! Honey! They're licking my ass!"

"Your wife seems like a little anal whore. Maybe we should change positions and see how many men it takes to fill your wife's asshole? What do you think of that? Squirm all you want, dude. We're tearing that hole up tonight."

"Oh Jesus...what are you doing to me now?"

"Now our boy's going to lie down in front of you. Sit your ass down on his cock. Do it!"

"Ohhhhoo....oh my God, baby. These boys want to fuck my ass!"

"That's right. We're going to see how many young cocks it takes to fill your wife's tight ass."

"Ohhhhh...it's so tight..."

"Now Sam's going to hump her from the back. He's going to stick his cock in your wife's dirty asshole and fill up that extra space."

"Oh my God! My ass is being stretched out! Oh, baby! It feels so good! I wish you could see this!"

"Now then. Here's the big test of just how wide your wife's asshole can stretch. Our boy Jessie is going to climb on top of your wife's back. There's just a little bit of asshole left. Now if he positions himself just right, he's going to fit his cock right in there and we're going to go for a wifey record."

"Oh fuck! H-Honey! Oh gawwwd they're fucking my ass! I can feel three cocks on my tight hole! Ohhh shit! I think I'm gonna cum!"

"Fuck her, goddamn it!"

"Ohhhhhhhh! Oh God, my ass is spasming! What are you doing to me?! Oh shiiiiit I'm cumming! I'm cumming!"

"Now wasn't that hard to listen to? But we're not done, old man. No, we got one more present for your dumb slut of a wife. We're going to cream pie that pussy and leave our dripping cum all over her. What do you think of that?"

"Ohhhhhhh yeah. Honey they're pulling out of me. My ass is gaping. My hole is so huge now..."

"Now we studs are going to take turns cumming inside of your wife's pussy. Sure hope she's on the pill because I didn't bring any condoms. Sam is up first. He's as horny as hell, because he's fucking her pussy like a madman."

"Ohhhhhhh yeah! Fuck me little boy! Ohhh yeah! Give me your cum!"

"Wooo! That was a good one. Jessie's up next. Think she can take another cumshot?"

"Oh Jessie! Oh Honey, I like it...ohh yeah. Ohhh! He's pounding that cock into me! Ohhh yeah, spray it! Spray it!"

"Alan's up to bat now. Damn, that boy sure doesn't know the meaning of the word gentle. He just wants a place to fire his cum. Your wife makes a good incubator."

"Oh he's cumming in meeeee! Ohh honey...I have so much cum in me...you have to see this."

"Why not? Take the old guy's blindfold

off. I want him to see me fuck his wife's dirty pussy."

"Hey honey! I can see you again. You like what you see? Huh? Ohhh Jerry's cock is the best. It's so huge. And he knows just how I like it."

"Take a good look, hubby. I want you to see what a cum-covered whore your wife turned out to be."

"Ohhhh Jesus! Yeah! Cum in me! Oh, God please cum in me, I can't take any more of this! My pussy is getting sore!"

"Hear that, man? Your wife's cunt is all worn out. Glad to be of service. Maybe she'll start treating you better now! HAH!"

"Ohhhh cum inside me, Jerry! Squirt it inside me! Ohhhhh yeah! Give me that sperm! Every! Last! Drop! Mmmmm..."

"Well, old man. Sorry to fuck and run. But we got to hit a movie tonight. Thanks for letting us fuck up your old lady. And hey...grow some balls, man. Okay?"

"Ohhhh...ohhhh...honey. The guys have all left. Did you pass out? I don't blame you. I feel like passing out myself. My asshole is huge and my pussy has four loads of dripping cum still inside. This was a great birthday present."

"And I must say, even though you messed up once. You really proved to be a good boy at the end. I guess you really do love me."

"Yes...I do."

"And guess what? Even though you don't deserve it, I think I'm going to be nice to my dear sweet hubby and give you the present I promised you."

"You mean...?"

"Yes. You tried your best. You failed, as usual, but you did try. And for that, you get an extra special reward. You get to clean my pussy out with that wagging tongue of yours."

"Oh. Thank you, thank you, honey. I'm so happy!"

# 6 THE THREESOME FACE

The flirtation started all so innocently. It started with a comment, a look, an improper thought shared between two friends.

"Hey ya sweetheart," Larry said to Jennifer, as he stood outside the convenience store.

"Haven't seen you in a while. How have you been doing?" Larry said, looking a bit too closely at Jennifer's squirrely but still exotically sexy face.

"Okay, I guess," she said wistfully, enjoying the feeling of Larry looking at her in that way after so many years.

I don't blame her for eyeing Larry, my very attractive husband. He's over thirty now but he never lost that baby face. I always say Larry looks like a movie star, as he doesn't age; he just becomes fuller and stronger in his features. He has that Puerto Rican shaded skin and very dark and penetrating eyes. My personal favorite is his badass goatee, demonstrating just how unafraid he is to take on the world and do whatever or whoever.

"I'm doing okay," Larry said strongly. "Working like crazy. You know how that goes."

"And yet you still find time to mingle with your old friends. I'm honored!" she laughed.

Larry loves wearing his sunglasses outdoors so it's hard to imagine poor lonely Jennifer not feeling some little attraction. I do wonder though which one made the first move and which one of them just played along.

"Oh come on. You know you've always been a good friend to me, Jen...to us," he clarified, speaking of his neglected-to-mention wife.

"You too Larry, you've always been such a good friend."

"Well, I'm not usually nice to anyone. But you got to keep your friends close, you know what I mean?"

"Sure!"

"I mean, honestly, most people are just walking, talking clumps of shit," Larry candidly remarked, much to Jennifer's exuberance.

"Larry! So bad!"

"Well, we got to admit it sometimes. I mean we both work. We deal with assholes all day long, right?"

"Well, yes we do. I try to be nice though," she said with a cute little head bob.

"See, I've given up on the whole 'being nice just to be nice' thing. I think respect is earned. Like you, we respect each other because we're both decent human beings."

I can just see Jennifer smirking, rolling her eyes so subtly, sending her starry eyes upward in deep thought—or should I say in pretend deep thought, so as to attract the attention of my very excitable husband.

"I don't know. I guess I do feel that way sometimes. Maybe I should come to the dark side with you...get some anger out. But I'm too much of a good girl," she said with a little flutter of her eyelashes.

"You were always a good girl," Larry said evenly before adding a smarmy retort. "The dark side is fun sometimes. You can't be a good Catholic schoolgirl your whole life!"

"I am not Catholic," Jennifer replied with a snarl. "And I'm almost as old as you are, buddy. So don't try that 'little girl' act on me!"

Oh yes, they were definitely flirting, and I don't know who started it. I know that

Larry can be a gawker and that he thinks about fucking every woman he sees regardless of her age or disposition. Then again, I always suspected Jennifer was a little slut, hiding behind all that "I found Jesus" bullshit that she posts on Facebook.

I certainly can't blame Larry for looking. Jennifer had a very exotic quality about her. She had a gypsy face for sure, with beady little eyes and a foxy smile. She had mordant eyes and eyebrows, and she always smiled big for the camera with a closed mouth—as if she was hiding something. Or maybe it was a self-conscious smile to protect her teeth—or metaphorically speaking, her pearly whites.

She certainly had a nice body, I'll give her that. Back when Larry and Jennifer were single, she used to have a doughy figure. But she has been working out consistently for the last few years and lost some of the chub. Now she couldn't help but show off her assets, accentuating her big breasts and her very long legs. Yes, she was a giant all right, standing over the head of most guys at a pretty impressive five foot eleven inches. Her hair, dyed blonde but oh so pretty, was also a head-turner.

Poor Larry! He never did get to fuck a giant. But he did confess a while back just how close he came to sampling Jennifer's exotic beauty.

"We never had sex. Sadly. I mean you and I weren't together back then...," he said cautiously.

"I know, I know," I laughed.

"Not that I didn't want to. But well, I don't know. Back then, we were different people. I wasn't the suave, confident romantic hero I am now," he said to my amusement. "And Jen, well, Jen was just all over the place, in love with two other guys. I just think we had bad timing."

"So nothing ever happened," I asked, raising my eyebrow.

"Well...."

"Aha! I knew something must have happened."

"We had cybersex once," Larry confessed nervously, though with a little happy glow in his smile.

"Really?"

"Yeah. Neither of us really liked talking on the phone. But we both happened to be online one day...."

"Yeah?"

"And she seduced me."

I laughed out loud, just visualizing Jennifer's passive aggressive sexy come-on's and Larry's half-hearted flirt-backs.

"And what happened?"

"Well," Larry said excitedly, shifting around on the couch, obviously tickled pink at my indulging about his almost-score. "It was pretty twisted actually. We both did a little role-playing. I was the aggressive guy, the master, and she was the sub. She had a 'forced' fantasy and I played my role to the tee. I couldn't believe the stuff that was coming out of my mouth, or my text, to be honest."

"And did you two touch yourselves?"

"She claimed to have orgasmed just from the fantasy I gave her. Even without touching herself."

"Hmm, well you are pretty creative when you want to be. I wouldn't be surprised."

"Yeah, she's a sweetheart. I guess it was just one of those things that didn't work out."

"Mmm-hmm," I said, feeling a bit of the green-eyed monster.

"Now, of course, she's with Ed."

"Ah yes, Ed."

Ed, her old man of a boyfriend, probably 20 or 30 years her senior. Larry can't help but be provoked by Ed's very existence. The woman he could have scored with years ago, settling for someone so "out of her league." I found Larry's inexplicable dislike of Ed rather charming. I didn't have to wonder; I knew exactly what he was feeling, if not thinking. He regretted letting Jennifer get away. And in the back of his mind, he wondered what a one-time fling would have felt like. Would it have been as hot as his cybersex fantasy?

I guess he would never know.

"Larry, I am officially old!" Jennifer told my husband, meeting him again at a gas station and shooting the breeze as friends tend to do—friends whom, you know, secretly lust each other behind platonic hugs. "I went through a drive-thru the other day, and a 17-year-old girl waited on me and, while giving me my food, asked if I was her classmate's mother. Her mother! I almost cried."

"Ouch," Larry replied with a giggle.

"It's not funny! I couldn't say anything back. I was in total shock. I mean, I guess it would be possible to have a kid at my age...but I would have given birth at like twelve! I mean what the heck?"

"I know how that goes. It hurts now that cashiers don't even bother checking my ID anymore. They just turn and give me a half look and ring up my alcohol. That's depressing."

"Ha ha, at least no one suggested you were someone's father!"

"True. That was pretty cold. You should have smacked her one."

Jennifer cackled, "Oh, believe me, I

wanted to. But she said it so innocently...."

"Ah...that fake innocence," Larry commented, leering at Jennifer's cross necklace and her deceptively conservative dress. "You've got to watch out for that."

"You be sure to tell Hannah...."

Yes, his wife, as I'm sure they both remembered at the same time.

"To enjoy her last couple of years as a twenty-year-old. It goes by so fast...much quicker than you imagine. Now that I'm 30, I keep thinking, 'Oh my God...I'm only ten years away from being 40!'"

"Me too! Our generation was not meant to get old," Larry snickered.

"Well, I guess I should be leaving, Larry," Jennifer said, always one to gratuitously mention Larry's name aloud, as if subliminally calling to him.

"We should talk more often though," Jennifer conspicuously suggested.

To which Larry replied, "Sure...I'm still on Yeehaw Messenger," no doubt thinking of the last time he cyber-fucked her.

"Larry," Jennifer said in a very concerned tone. "I...I...have a bit of a confession to make."

"Oh, what is it?" he asked very innocently, as if he really didn't know.

"I still think about you...that time online...you know what I mean."

"Oh...," Larry said, probably not

expecting Jennifer's bluntness.

"That was a long time ago."

"Yes, I know. And I'm with Ed now."

"Right, right...."

"And I really don't know what's going to become of Ed and me. I mean...can you imagine what it's like being stuck with someone who's always miserable...who never wants to go anywhere or do anything?"

"Hmmm," Larry said, a bit confused, most likely ogling at Jennifer's fabulous tits.

"And to make things worse, he mocks my faith. And my faith is very important to me."

"Well, yeah. I understand that. Umm...but I don't understand why you're telling me this."

"I guess because...I always wondered what it would be like. You know, if we had gotten together. I know Hannah is great and all. Maybe it's just me. I have stupid fantasies. Bye Larry."

"Wait, wait!" Larry said, always so eager to protect the feelings of vulnerable women. "Look, Jen...you know we'll always be friends."

"I know."

"And of course I still...think about those days. It's natural. And I am very, very...very...very tempted," he said oh so prudently, as he gazed at her cross necklace just wondering how he could defile her.

Jennifer giggled.

"But you know I love my wife. She's put up with me for a long time. My crazy mood swings and workaholic lifestyle. The only good thing about me is the fact that I'm faithful to her and she deserves every part of me."

"That's very sweet, Larry," Jennifer said with a bittersweet smile.

"And if things were different and I had ended up with you, I would be saying the same thing to Hannah. I honor vows. I guess I'm old-fashioned that way."

"Yes, you are old-fashioned...but it's a very good old-fashioned way about you, Larry."

"So that's my policy. My dick belongs to my wife."

Jennifer laughed hard. "And does she lend it out? At parties and such?"

"Umm, I don't think so," Larry laughed weakly, perturbed at Jen's creepy implication.

"I guess I never asked."

"Well, have a good week, Larry," Jennifer said with a coy look.

"And that was it, huh?" I asked my blushing babe.

"Of course, I have no secrets. I figured you deserve full exposure."

"And were you tempted?"

"Well, of course, I was! You know the male sex drive is an uncontrollable animal just waiting to be unleashed. I have to store my rage behind a cage."

I laughed it off.

"But oh well...old memories."

"Hmm...how forward of her. The question is...," I toyed with Larry, giving him a sharp-bladed look, "would you go for it if I let you?"

"What do you mean?"

"You know. If I let you...would you have sex with Jennifer? For old time's sake?"

He laughed and thought it over. "Well...is there really a safe answer for that?"

"There's an honest answer. So what is it?"

"Honey...I would never in a million years cheat on you. But if you're asking me if I would have sex with Jen, no strings attached, well Jesus...I'm not made of stone."

"Hmm, interesting," I said with a pout and a smile.

"But hey, you know, there's no sense in you staying home while I have fun. So I guess I would have to tell Jen that the only way it could happen is if both you and I could play."

I laughed hard and dropped my jaw in flattered surprise. "Me and Jen? All three of us. Wouldn't I have to...you know...swing both ways to do that?"

"Maybe. Or you could both service my cock."

I guffawed. "The sultan of cock!"

"Yeah, that's right. That's how they do it in Arabia."

"And are there Arabian princesses who get double the cock?"

"Only the really sexy ones...," he teased, kissing me and igniting an intense night of lovemaking.

After we shed our clothes and embraced, we began to indulge each other with fantasies. He gave me my fantasy of two well-hung Arabians gangbanging me, making me cum twice. When it was his turn to cum, I decided to give him an extra special treat.

"Maybe your perfect night would start with me bringing home a house guest. Maybe someone like...hmm...Jen? And I would say, 'She's your birthday present. We both are.'"

"Mmm yeah," he mumbled as I stroked his hard cock.

"And maybe we'd get undressed for you and let you play with our tits. Hmm? Or would you prefer we both take turns in sucking your cock?"

"Yes!" Larry exclaimed while I swallowed

his hard dick and licked it up.

"You like when I suck you?" I said, wet stroking his cock with my spit. "Or maybe you prefer Jen's lips. Maybe she sucks nice and slow...like a good, subservient little girl."

I sucked his head slowly and delicately, tasting him and wiggling my tongue.

It didn't take long for him to cum after my fantasy. But it did get us both thinking. Just what would a threesome with Jennifer feel like? Would it ruin our marriage? Would it cause lots of drama? Or maybe it would just be a harmless fantasy come to life. I could give my husband the horny fantasy he never claimed...and, at the same time, conquer my inhibitions of pleasuring another woman.

"Hmmm...do you think our minds are in the gutter for even thinking about this?" I asked my husband, who waited nervously on the opposite end of the table.

We decided to journey to Redd's Café for our anniversary dinner. I wore my blue three-quarter polyester sleeve dress. My husband wore a nice black suit and light blue shirt. And Jennifer, our mysterious "date" for our anniversary dinner, wore a blue and turquoise dress with a blue sweater. We were all draped in blue! I figure it was because we all felt friendly, artistic, and inspired. Or, maybe we were all moping around? I don't know, but all Larry and I was thinking all night, as we ordered more drinks and exchanged funny stories, was how much it would be to dress in each other's clothes.

Jennifer was a good sport, and I'm not sure if she realized at that point why we invited her along. Maybe she figured we were bored. Maybe she was anticipating a bit of jealousy on my part. I don't know, but come on, Jen... You had to know something was up? What couple celebrates their anniversary with a friend? Unless, of course, that couple wants you as their anniversary present....

Jennifer smiled at both of us; she grinned for a couple of hours. At any given point, she was gazing at Larry or me, listening intently to every word and gutturally giggling as if she had a schoolgirl crush.

Larry and I wondered if she had the face—you know, the threesome face—that would let us know it's okay to ask her. I couldn't believe how awkward it felt...considering that we used to do this all the time when we were single and asking for one on dates. What is it about being a married couple that makes it feel...creepy?

Jennifer excused herself twice that night and went to the bathroom, shaking her ass to our amusement.

"What should we do now?" Larry asked.

"Maybe we should just come out and tell her."

"But won't she feel pressured? As if we paid her way just to get her into bed?"

"All she can say is no," I shrugged.

"But how do we ask?"

"Let's invite her back to our place!" I volunteered. We both giggled to ourselves when we say Jennifer coming back to the table, thinking the unmentionable and enjoying our champagne.

"What's so funny?" Jennifer asked with a sneer.

"Just talking about you," I said with a polite smile.

Suddenly, the stakes were up. "We were just talking about how beautiful you look tonight, Jen," Larry said boldly. "How beautiful you always have been. Maybe it's the wine talking. But we just aren't ready to say goodnight yet."

Jennifer slowly turned to meet my face, wondering if I would be fuming or shooting daggers at Larry. To her surprise, I was just staring back at her, smiling and wondering what lay behind that adorable little dress.

Jennifer blushed and took turns looking at us both. "Well...," she giggled and hid her face, "do you know what you're saying?"

We all mirrored her shyness and giggled. We all went for another drink. Larry kept staring at Jennifer, as did I. Maybe we didn't have the guts to say what we wanted, but we were all thinking it. And I'm pretty sure that Jennifer had the threesome face by the time the night was over.

We all entered the bedroom at our place and sat on the master bed, awkwardly trading glances and feeling the blanket's velvety embrace.

Everyone seemed to be waiting for someone else to take the lead. Finally, I spoke up, simply sharing a thought.

"So...Jen...Larry tells me you two had quite the steamy affair a few years ago...via messenger?"

Larry and Jen cracked up and shifted around in the bed.

"So tell me, what was it like?"

"It involved a little...ummm...BDSM. I was the master. She was my slave...and was forced to pleasure me," Larry giggled.

"And do you still like to be the slave, Jen?"

"Mmm-hmm," she said softly, meeting my eyes and holding the thought.

"Kiss her, Larry."

They both looked at each other and hesitated.

"I insist. Your wife is giving you an order."

Jennifer and Larry both sat closer to one another and both glanced at me for the go-ahead. When they finally locked lips, I felt a surge of jealousy come over me...but I held onto it and let it fester.

The more he kissed her and sinned in my presence, the more turned on Jennifer became. I could hear her voice crack and wheeze—just his firm lips alone were taking her breath away. Oh yes...I could tell she was going to be a loud one.

"Undress her."

Larry laughed and Jennifer resisted, which only started to annoy me.

I lost my smile and insisted. "I said undress her."

I glared at Jennifer and that stupid little necklace of hers. "I want you to undress this little slut."

Jennifer looked back at me in hurt, but it very quickly turned into a submissive spirit when Larry obliged and grabbed her by the shoulders. He forcefully took her sweater off, leaving Jennifer speechless and ready to be violated.

"Take her clothes off. Do it," I commanded Larry as he politely put his hands on her dress. "Take it off."

He grabbed the shoulders and forcefully pulled the dress down, exposing Jennifer's shoulders. She sighed as Larry pulled down her dress to her waist, exposing her sexy black underwire bra.

"Don't just look at her. Fuck her. It's what you two have been wanting, isn't it?" I asked harshly, playing the role of insanely jealous housewife to a 'T'.

Jennifer panted as Larry grabbed her delicate frame and laid his body weight on her.

"Oh...," Jennifer exhaled, feeling Larry's steamy kisses all over her chest. He kissed her with fire, surrendering to his temptation after so many years of polite conversation. Jennifer was so turned on she could hardly keep her eyes open. The only time she opened them was to look back at me, praying that I was enjoying myself. Maybe I was, maybe I wasn't, but that wasn't her concern. I ordered my husband to fuck, and he was going to follow orders.

Larry sat up and pulled Jennifer's pull-down dress all the way past her waist and down to her ankles and feet. He looked up at her beautiful body, now only clothed by a bra and black lace boy short panties.

I leaned over closer towards the bouncing side of the bed, as Larry lowered himself down to Jen's chest so he could kiss her yummy belly.

"Ohh...," Jennifer replied self-consciously, always looking up to me, looking for guidance.

"Take her bra off," I scolded Larry, wanting to see Jennifer's big tits, the ones he fantasized about for God knows how many nights.

"Sit up," I commanded, halting Jennifer's hands. "I want him to take it off."

Jennifer looked at Larry in anticipation as Larry moved his hands behind her and unfastened her bra. When he pulled those lacey straps off, her beautiful natural breasts bounced out of there in a hurry.

I felt just as turned on as Larry, as he devoured those melons with his hungry mouth. Jennifer groaned in pleasure as he sucked those perky but exotically dark nipples.

"Oh yeah...," Jennifer mumbled while looking up at me in surrender. "Hurt me."

"What's that?"

"Pinch them...," she cooed, signaling to me that we were being far too nice to this bad Catholic schoolgirl.

"Like this?" I asked as I pinched her happy nipple and shot her tit around.

"Oh God, yes!" she squealed.

"You like that, you little slut?"

"Yes!" she gasped.

I moved closer to her for a better angle and position so that I could abuse those big nasty titties. I squeezed both of her nipples at the same time while Larry started kissing her thighs, working his way up to her panties.

"Oh God...," Jennifer whimpered.

"You like that, huh?" I slapped her tits hard, firming her nipple and alarming her.

"Yes!"

"Shut up! You're just here to suffer."

"Yes...."

"Eyeing my husband. Shaking your big tits at him. I think you just want to be punished, you little whore."

Larry pulled her panties off, treating us both to that nicely shaved bush.

"Wait," I said to Larry.

"Spread your dirty pussy, Jennifer."

"Uh huh...," she mewled; spreading her labia for Larry's viewing pleasure.

"How do you feel, Jen?" Larry snidely barked.

"Like a sluuuut!" Jennifer screamed, as Larry found her bulging clit and started tonguing it.

"You sure look like a slut," I said, as I continued pinching and slapping her sensitive spots for her sins. Larry meanwhile sucked on that clit like a madman, getting to taste the pussy he missed out on.

Oh yes, Larry. Taste every lick and every secretion, I remember thinking. She is my present to you...to us both.

"I want you to suck his cock now, Jennifer. You hear that?"

"Yeah...."

"That's what you've been wanting to do the last five years, right?"

"Yes."

"Why is that?"

"Because I'm a whore...."

Larry unbuckled his belt and unzipped his pants, but Jennifer stared only at me. I knew exactly what she was thinking—no, not thinking: feeling. I knew what she was feeling. She thought this was wrong...but everything felt right. She craved the abuse. She yearned for the guilt complex. Oh, yeah, I was going to give it to her.

"Lay her down on the bed. That's how prostitutes are supposed to do it."

Larry sent me a look as if to say, "Gee Honey...aren't you taking it a bit far?" But I'm pretty sure I was playing the game Jen wanted.

"Take that off," I said, offering Jennifer the chance to remove the cross necklace and sink deeper into our little role-playing game.

"No...," she said softly before ending with a smile, "leave it on."

"Why?"

"Because..."

"You're a little Christian slut?"

"Oh God, yeah!"

"Suck his cock, you whore!"

Larry stuffed Jennifer's panting mouth with his cock, leaning over her and sitting on his knees. It was such a turn-on to see Jennifer's big mouth and hear her annoying voice finally shut up for once and in the most glorious of ways. Larry was as horny as a toad and made sure she sucked on that cock with little to no time for breathing. Whenever she wasn't sucking his head, he was face fucking her to oblivion. He pounded the back of her throat as if it were a G-spot, forcing tears out of Jen's eyes. When he withdrew, Jennifer gasped for air and shrieked in orgasmic frenzy.

I crawled over to the other side of the bed and laid across her feet, rendering her immobile and helpless. I selfishly wanted a piece of that perfect pussy. I started slowly at first, rubbing her muff and finding her clit.

"Ohhhh gggaaahhh," she mumbled, filled with my husband's leaking manhood. Oh but she felt every rub, every finger fuck I had to give her.

"What's the matter?" Larry said, withdrawing from her mouth and shoving his dick all over her cheeks. "Can't breathe?"

She panted and gasped for air, begging for more of her master's cock.

"Maybe there's just too much for you to handle."

"I know…I'm just a worthless slut," Jennifer sighed.

"Maybe Hannah should show you how to suck a cock right."

An invitation! I was so turned on I couldn't help but rise to my sultan's call. I crawled over Jen and to my husband. He lay comfortable on his back and invited me over to his smooth, glistening erection.

I grabbed that pole and sucked the life out of it, stroking it and sucking it without pity.

"Ohhh God!" he wailed and the popping sounds continued.

Jennifer waited in silent loyalty, waiting for her next command and pinching her nipples like the bad girl we knew she was. Jennifer slowly crawled over to the opposite side of me so she could get a close-up view of my husband's hard dick and my fast, virtually motorized mouth.

"Is this what you were thinking about, whore?" I yelled at Jen, sucking his cock in aggression, taunting her to compete.

"Yes…please, please, I want it…."

Jennifer grabbed the cock out of my hand and sucked on it twice as hard, eyeing me the whole time.

"Ohhh," the lucky bastard said as we took turns in choking on his rod.

"You want to be like me, Jen?" I asked the little slut, staring a hole through her face.

"Yeah...I want everything you have, Hannah."

"Lick his cock with me. I want to lick your lips across my husband's dick."

"Oh yeah...."

Larry was a mumbling mess by this point as we both French kissed in between his aching cock. Jennifer's lips were sweet and the perfect aftertaste to Larry's salty dong. When she licked the shaft, I licked the head. When I nibbled the shaft, she licked his prick hole with vengeance. We both tried to swallow the head at the same time and shared a romantic kiss.

"Oh fuck! I'm coming!" Larry screamed.

I grabbed Jennifer by the hair and made sure Larry shot his cum load all over her pretty little whore face. As I watched Jennifer's face get creamed with jizz, I finally saw what Larry saw in her. She was fucking beautiful.

"Spphtt!" Jennifer said, spitting the cum from her lips and backing away from us on the bed.

The role-play was over, and truthfully, I did feel a tad guilty at how far I took our game. I hoped she didn't take offense to me repeatedly calling her a slut. And Larry...well fuck, Larry better not has any complaints about anything.

I giggled to myself, sounding a bit sheepish. "Wow," I laughed. "Are you okay?"

Jennifer pouted and went towards the bathroom to wash her tainted face.

"You two are pigs!" she snarled.

Larry and I looked at each other in surprise. I supposed we were a tad rough on her. But for my first threesome experience, I couldn't have asked for a hotter night.

"Sorry...just in the moment, you know," I said with a shy giggle.

"Well, there's no excuse for that behavior!" Jennifer yelled from the bathroom.

"I guess we need a safe word," Larry replied.

I couldn't help but giggle at the whole thing. So what if I'm aggressive? She wanted to fuck my husband.... I just gave her what she wanted! Hmm...maybe a little more than what she wanted....

Jennifer emerged from the bathroom with a clean face and with something she grabbed from her purse.

"Now it's your turn, Hannah!" Jennifer smiled wickedly and held up a pair of handcuffs meant for me, all the while wearing that shameful necklace and playing the role of the bad, bad girl.

"It's time for you to learn some manners...," she shook her shoulders side to side, taunting me and exposing those bouncy breasts to us both.

Jennifer and Larry smiled at me and

enjoyed my shit-eating grin. Oh, boy...this was going to be one hard lesson all right....

# 7 THE SOFT SWAP

The idea of partner swapping was completely foreign to me for most of my life. I was raised Protestant and my husband Aaron was Catholic. After sorting out all of those complicated issues, we were relieved to live a somewhat quiet and normal life.

The very idea of being "unfaithful" was associated with infidelity, with leaving your spouse and joining the "world". Abandoning a family. Betraying someone's trust. The very idea of a committed but loose relationship just didn't make sense to anyone in my family.

When we first met Layla and Rico, we had no idea they were swingers, or what the term swinger even meant. We met them in an online couple's chat room—a regular, G-rated chat room—and they both bought us a "virtual drink". We didn't actually think of it as a, "Hey I'm buying you a drink!" scenario. We thought it to be more along the lines of "Hey, we're all really bored. Let's go have coffee in 'real life' someday." We thought about Layla and Rico, Fred and Ethel. Being work at home professionals, my husband and I didn't get out of the house much, and so we were fairly oblivious to all the signals going around online.

Aaron, being the stalker he is, decided to search for both of their email addresses on a search engine. We saw the word "swinger" in his and her profile but we had no idea what it meant. We thought it meant something to do with golf! So the next time I chatted with Layla online, and she didn't bring up what "swinger" meant, we all but forgot about it.

Now that I look back though, I did think something odd of Layla's email follow up.

So describe to me what you look like, Savannah. I'll go first. ? I am about thirty, Hispanic and have black hair. I have a thin waist and hourglass figure. People usually compliment my eyes. They're not really big, just very excitable and I do tend to look at people when I talk to them. That's why I have the reputation of having adorable eyes. LOL My husband is thirty-two and is in tiptop shape, he being a bit of an exercise junkie. He has an adorable face with strong eyes, big eyelashes and wonderful lips. Oh yeah and he also has a very nice singing voice. We are sociable and do occasionally go to clubs. But lately, we find ourselves just hanging around the house. Things do get lonely, since our other friends moved out of state. So we sometimes go online to see what trouble we can start. ? Write me back and tell me a little bit about yourself.

All right, I admit I am a bit of a ditz sometimes. I had NO idea what she was implying with that message. I thought it was cute that she was so friendly and so willing to share details of her life. I never quite got that she was "selling" herself or "qualifying me." Now that I look back, I can see subtle hints...indicating that she was proud of her body, and was expecting me to have an "average physique", if you get my drift. (And apparently, I never got that drift!)

Like a klutz, I wrote back and sidestepped everything she talked about, opening up in probably the worst way possible.

I must say, I'm a bit of a crazy cat lady! LOL We have two cats and no children. We don't really want children. We're vegetarian. We don't really workout, so I'm not sure we're the type to play volleyball with you. We sort of keep to ourselves. We don't go clubbing. We were raised in a religious household, but we aren't really active anymore. We like to read. As far as flaws, I think I tend to be very anal. My husband Aaron is a bit of a bottom sometimes. LOL We should meet up sometime. We are bored on weekends and always looking to meet new people. PS You sound very cute!

Yes, the foot-in-mouth award goes to Savannah! Now that I look back and realize what she was really asking, I shudder. I avoided the topic of appearance, and actually said I was anal and my husband was a bottom. Call it my crazy way of talking...I always just used the word bottom and "ass" interchangeable. As in, my husband is being a bottom and is super-cranky today. Apparently, a "bottom" means something in the swinger world.

No wonder Layla was tickled pink at my reply.

You have the cutest way of expressing yourself! I am surprised to hear that you're "anal" and that your husband um...swings that! Rico doesn't sadly. He's the alpha chimp. I like your honesty, Savannah. Which is why I'm wondering why you're not being honest about what you look like. A lot of people think that I'm superficial and judge other people by their appearances. That's not what I'm like at all. But I expect people to be honest about their body shapes. I am very forward with who I am, as you might notice. So don't be shy. Tell me what you and your hubby look like. I really like you. You're very weird, but in a good way. ? I can tell you have a lively sense of humor.

I did think it was strange that Layla was focusing on appearances, when in my mind appearances did not matter at all. And sex wasn't even an issue! But she was determined to put a face to her fantasy. I did feel strange about describing my looks...but attributed her interest to curiosity. As in, how do I know it's you when we finally meet at the mall together?

Well, Layla since you *really* want to know...? I am a natural redhead. I am a bit tall and lanky. I'm not thin anymore, but I'd say I'm average. My husband and are both in our mid-thirties. He's uh...a guy? Hahah...not sure how to describe a handsome guy. He sort of looks like Daniel Craig, that same sort of British machismo. But he's not British. He's pasty white though LOL No, I think we're just regular looking people. Why? Is this some weird thing where you can only be friends with someone in your league?

Layla responded quickly, and seemed very enthused.

Wow, Savvy. A *natural* redhead. I am very much looking forward to seeing proof of this. Tee hee! What an odd description of your husband. I was laughing quite a bit upon reading it. How big is he, by the way? Seriously, please don't think I'm one of those people who takes appearances so seriously. I really just like the "soul" of a person. My husband feels the same way. We see beauty within and without. And sometimes a person is most beautiful inside. And sometimes exploring a person's beauty "inside" is a lot of fun. Tee hee!

Again, paint me stupid. I didn't see anything strange about the last message, and so answered like a complete bimbo.

LOL Well, I guess when we meet in person you'll see proof right away that I'm a real redhead. How big is Aaron? I don't know about six feet I guess. Although I'm actually taller than him! Heh. And I agree, there is beauty in everything and everyone. I suppose finding beauty in everyone and everything is fun. Speaking of fun, we should meet sometime.

As you can imagine, disaster was to follow. Layla and Rico were so captivated by my oblivious introduction they insisted that we come to their house and sample their dinner. They remembered our vegetarian diet so cooked for us a very elaborate meal.

All right, by then I started to think something was up. Who goes through so much effort just to have a fun night with new friends?

Of course, I was thinking they were salespeople or religious cooks. Aaron, however, was starting to figure it out by now. To his credit, he figured out their not-so-hidden "secret" within a few minutes.

Aaron and I shook hands with our new friends and entered their lavish home. After a few pleasantries, we sat down on their leather sectional and relaxed.

Aaron was already feeling uneasy and so started the conversation on an ambiguous note. "So...how exactly did we meet again?" He laughed nervously.

Rico answered happily. "We first met in the couples chat room, remember?"

"Ohhh right, that was you," Aaron nodded. "That's cool. And then...?"

Layla chimed in, "Savannah and I started emailing each other. And we hit it off."

"Ohh," Aaron replied blankly.

However, he was startled when Rico winked at him and nodded.

"Ummm...good, I guess. So what do you do for work, Rico?"

Rico replied casually, "I'm in the entertainment industry."

"Oh what do you do?"

"I run an escort service."

"What?" I cracked up, thinking Rico was

pulling our leg.

"Ah," Aaron replied uncertainly.

When I calmed down, the group stared at me. "Hon, he's not kidding."

"What?" I asked quite scandalized.

"Yeah. I founded the company about ten years ago. Living so close to Nevada, the competition is intense. But I think I've found an angle that works."

I cleared my throat. "Well, all right then! So...let's talk about my job! I'm an editor," I laughed nervously.

"Wait a minute," Rico said, leaning forward. "I think something is wrong here. Savannah, let me ask you something. Do you swing?"

"Swing? I used to. When I was a teenager!"

"Honey," Aaron grumbled. "They are asking us if we wife-swap."

"What?"

Layla and Rico looked at each other and giggled.

"What do you mean?"

"They are swingers, Savvy. They have an 'open relationship.'"

"Oh...as in..."

"They want to sleep with you, Savvy," Aaron said nonchalantly, figuring the night couldn't get any more awkward.

"Oh...my God!" I said in mortified embarrassment.

"But I'm married!" I chortled.

"So are we," Layla replied.

"You...oh my God. I am so sorry..."

Rico and Layla nodded in acceptance.

"It's okay. That does explain why we were miscommunicating in our email conversations," Layla pointed out. "I just figured you were acquainted with the lifestyle when you said your husband was a bottom.

"Oh my God!" I said, standing up and experiencing a minor freak out. "I said I was anal. Oh my God," I laughed myself till I was red in the face.

"I assure you she's not," nodded Aaron. "And good to know that you called me a bottom, hon."

"This is a terrible misunderstanding! I'm so sorry!"

Rico held his hand up. "Say no more. We are disappointed. But the night is not lost. We still have a meal to provide," he nodded forcefully.

"I...golly gee!" I giggled, half horrified and half flattered. "I can't believe I didn't see this all along. I'm so stupid sometimes."

"Noo," Layla corrected me. "Don't ever think that. It's just a miscommunication, that's all."

"Yes, let's try to put this behind us, shall we?" Aaron said, trying to stay mature about the whole thing.

And try though we did, it was just

impossible not to talk about sex, once Pandora's Box had been opened.

"So...you two have sex with whoever you want?" I asked, probably being a tad rude.

"No, honey," Layla replied. "We only have fun with people we like. We are actually quite selective in who we play with."

"So...when you do...I mean...how do you do it?"

Layla laughed and shook her head. "Well...whatever a woman likes. Oral pleasure, some light anal play..."

"Oh!" I interrupted. "That's not what I meant. I just meant...you're bisexual?"

"Yes," Layla answered.

"I'm straight though," Rico said, looking at Aaron.

"No worries," he retorted.

"I'm sorry if I sound rude. I've just never met any 'swingers' before."

"It's okay. My husband did warn me that we might be 'robbing the cradle.' I guess he was right."

"But I'm older than you."

"Yes, but you're very green. A newbie, as they call you."

"Oh, I see."

We had some more drinks—a lot of drinks actually, to relieve the tension— and eventually accepted Rico and Layla's odd lifestyle. I guess I was proud of myself that I was able to stay platonic friends with a couple of swingers, and not judge them or hurt their feelings.

By the time we left the dining room table and journeyed to the couch, the conversation became a bit goofy. Aaron found himself seated closest to Layla, while I found myself sitting next to Rico. We thought nothing of it, but now that I think back, it may have been a devious little plan orchestrated by a very persistent, very horny couple.

Rico and Layla wisely didn't push us. They simply provoked us into asking them more questions. They loved answering questions about their lifestyle and their past experiences and the more they shocked Aaron and me, the more fascinated we became.

"So your last birthday was a threesome with a prostitute?"

"Yes," Rico said. "We went to the Horny Rabbit Ranch in Vegas."

"But...please don't tell me any details!" I laughed. "All I want to know is...how do you protect yourself from disease?"

"If there's any doubt we use a rubber. Or we insist upon testing. Of course, sometimes you just have a good feeling about a person," Rico said with a wink.

I crossed my legs and nodded.

"So," Layla asked me, starry-eyed and quite innocent in a way, "Would you ever consider playing with us?"

I guffawed, as Aaron raised his eyebrows. "Um...we have never ever...never...even thought about that."

"We're actually quite boring," Aaron suggested. "We were each other's first loves. Met in high school. Married. A true love sort of thing."

"That's very romantic," Layla said merrily. "But...do you plan to go your whole lives without ever experiencing the love of another person?"

"I...I guess so."

Aaron shrugged as well.

"I don't mean to be cynical. But that just seems a bit sad. I believe we only live once. And condemning yourself to a life sentence of just one person...well, where is the variety in that? I think you can love one person but still enjoy sharing fruits between various partners. It makes you appreciate each other all the more so."

"Hmm," I replied. "I guess I've never really thought about it. I just don't think I could actually do that."

"But how can you be sure if you never allow yourself to try new things?"

I thought it over and laughed. Layla mirrored my giggly response, she apparently being so determined to be my first bisexual experience.

"I'm just shy. We're both shy. I don't think we could do that."

"It's okay, I understand," Layla said with acceptance. "We can still be friends."

Somehow, I doubted it. Underneath Layla's doll face and perfectly rehearsed statements, beat the heart of an ultra-competitive "alpha female." I think it's safe to say no one ever told Layla "no" her entire life.

Throughout the night, she wouldn't stop looking at me, and insisted upon offering me drink after drink, as if she was trying to conquer my defenses.

Aaron seemed carefree about the whole thing; who knows, maybe he bought into the swinger argument from the very beginning. Or maybe he just wanted to have sex with Layla. She was beautiful, I must admit. She looked almost too perfect; her long bob haircut was arranged perfectly and she had a perfect smile with movie star quality lips.

Layla wasn't giving up and insisted upon playing a game of truth or dare, as an "alternative" to her night of naughty fun that she had been looking forward to. Right away, I could tell her questions were going to be just as kinky as her dares.

"Have you ever fantasized about another woman?"

I thought it over. "Yes."

"Who?"

"That's two questions!" I yelled.

She giggled. "Come on, you have to be honest or the game doesn't work."

"You know what, Layla? Let's just skip this and give you exactly what I want," I said in bratty confidence. Layla looked at me and tightened her brow, probably resenting anyone who raised her voice to her. "I have fantasized about you. Okay? Are you happy? That doesn't mean anything is going to happen."

The men cackled and Layla seemed pleased by the tidbit.

"So?"

"Wow, that really makes me feel...mmm...turned on," she laughed.

"Okay. I have a proposition for you then. No strings attached. I want to offer you a soft swap."

"What is that?"

"It's when you simply watch two people make love in front of you. You don't have to do anything. But you get to experience the same passion, as it is happening right in front of you."

"Huh. You two would do that? And it wouldn't feel weird to you?"

"No. We enjoy it. We do it many times."

"But not with just anyone. Only the ones we find special," winked Rico.

"Well...I don't know."

"Consider it a test to see if you have a

swinging personality," Layla said with a wide-eyed smile. "If you don't feel anything, then you know. Lose nothing, gain nothing."

I laughed and shrugged at Aaron who shrugged back.

"It's like watching a homemade porno film," Aaron retorted.

"But so much better," she nodded.

Already feeling horny, Layla wasted no time in getting the action started.

"Trade places with me, Savannah."

Layla took my spot and sat next to her husband.

She crawled on top of him and sat on his lap. They kissed tenderly for a few moments, oblivious to the world around them, and yet very aware that they were stars of the show.

Layla slowly unbuttoned her blue embroidered blouse as Rico kissed her chest. How romantic that she never lost the attraction for her husband, but rather multiplied her affections by bringing other people to applaud their performance. The lifestyle made sense, even though I found myself resisting the notion of trying it myself.

Layla looked back at us both, the two of us now sitting on the couch, and watching in awkward and yet very captivated interest.

She took her blouse off and showed off her sexy black bra.

"I want to do this on the floor," she said, right before stepping off the couch and pushing her man to the ground. "That way I can look at Savvy and get her feedback." She crawled atop him and straddled him on the living room floor.

I smiled, and shook my head, not having any idea of what feedback or criticism to offer. A sexual performance...it's not really like a manuscript, is it?

Layla positioned herself directly across from me, so she could look at me and Aaron while she made love to Rico. But in her eyes, she was only looking at me.

Rico unsnapped her bra and let it fall to the floor.

Her breasts bounced as merrily as she did and were perfectly shaped orbs of beauty. Rico kissed and caressed her, taking the time to suck the nipples.

"Oh yeah..." she suspired. "I like when he sucks my nipples. It feels good," she said only to me. Do you like it when Aaron does that to you?"

"Yes..." I replied blankly.

"Me too," she sighed. "Take your pants off, sweetie. Show Savannah and Aaron the thunder from down under."

We all giggled, and Rico excitedly pulled his big penis out, anxious for our commentary.

"Go Rico!" Aaron laughed.

"Ohh, he's a big one."

"Yeah…" Layla moaned, inserting Rico's firm member underneath her skirt.

I looked closely and had to ask, "Are you not wearing any underwear, Layla?"

"Noooo…" she said with a long wheeze. "I never wear underwear when guests come over," she clarified. "Just in case, you know."

"In case what?" I asked indulging.

"In case a beautiful woman wants to lick my pussy," she replied with a big smile.

"Ah," I said, backing away, starting to feel nervous.

"Yeah!" Layla gasped, bouncing up and down on Rico's steady member.

Rico's face turned red with passion. Layla treated me to a full view of Rico's hard body, unbuttoning his shirt and showing us all his firm pecks and rock-like abs.

"Wow, you're so buff, Rico," I jested.

"He stays in shape so he can pleasure beautiful women. Like you, Savvy."

"Oh, you're too kind!"

"Come on the floor, Savvy."

"Oh, I don't think so."

"Come on, I just want to hold your hand

when I cum. So you can know what it feels like. Nothing more."

"Hmmm...what do you think, honey?"

Aaron laughed. "Go ahead. It's just like a handshake...with a slight physiological difference."

I played the good sport and nervously, cautiously, walked over to meet them both. I sat Indian style by Rico and next to Layla.

I had a big grin on my face, almost giggling, but Layla calmed me when she touched my shoulder.

"It feels so good when you touch me. I can feel the difference in the air," she said still gyrating on top of her devoted husband."

"So does Rico have sex with other women in front of you?"

"Sometimes. If I like her," Layla said, meeting my eyes.

"Hmm, good deal."

"Touch him, Savvy."

"Noo...I don't think so!"

"Come on. He won't bite."

"No. I'll touch you, Layla. That was the deal."

"Okay, I like that better anyway!"

I slowly put my hand out and touched Layla's body. I felt her smooth tummy and down to her hips. She had a beautiful shape; feminine, not too fit but just the right amount of curves.

"Hmmm, I love your hands," she cooed to me.

"Touch her ass!" Aaron heckled.

My friend and I giggled.

"Do it," she insisted. I'm very proud of my ass. I like when girls touch it."

I shook my head and humored her, feeling her, admittedly, very tight and proportioned butt.

Her backside was vibrating, bouncing up and down on Rico. I could smell her intimacy all over the room. It wasn't really offensive...it was actually a bit of a turn on. Maybe the smell of sex is a contagion, because I did feel the urge to have sex with Aaron—just to compete—just to make Layla feel special.

Layla stopped riding him and looked at me, grabbing my attention. "I want you to see this."

She crawled off of him and slithered lower to his knees, just enough so that she could give him a blowjob.

"Oh, now you're embarrassing me," I said shyly.

"Just watch me, sugar," Layla said, eyeing me and letting her tongue work it.

I giggled for a few moments, but eventually made peace with the fact that they were fearlessly making love in front of me, so proud of themselves—their bodies, their affection and their exquisitely high tastes.

I did want to do Layla a favor, so I leaned down and sat back right next to Rico. Rico leaned over smiled at me, enjoying his blowjob. But Layla was far more interested in me and looked into my eyes the whole time she was stroking and sucking.

Layla reached her hand over to put on my stomach. I looked at her hand and then back to her, giving her permission to touch me.

Her caress was very soft and non-threatening. It didn't feel like a greedy grab, but a soulful connection of sorts. She moved her hand softly across my tummy, atop my purple sweater blouse. She had a goal in mind, and gradually snuck her silky hand underneath my blouse, caressing my doughy and supple skin.

It felt really good. And the fact that another woman was touching me didn't seem bothersome. I didn't really know where to go from here, so I was glad that Layla simply allowed me permission to stand still and feel good.

"I want you to taste me,"

"Me?"

"I'd love it if you tasted me, sex kitty. But I was actually talking to my husband."

"Oh, I know," I giggled.

A grinning Rico obliged and sat up while she lied on her back. He mounted her, and sank his gentle kisses all the way down her chest and to her stomach. She lifted her skirt giving me and Rico a full view of her vagina and neatly trimmed pubic hair. I sat up for a better view of the action.

"Lick me...I want you to lick me while Savvy watches."

I giggled and watched in amazement as Rico eagerly licked his wife's clitoris, with not a worry in the world.

"And you too, Aaron," Layla reminded poor Aaron, who was almost forgotten while lurking in the background.

"Don't mind me, I'm enjoying the show."

"Your wife is very sexy, you know."

"I know. Lucky me. Is there anything you want to know about her?"

"Aaron!" I replied, slightly embarrassed.

"She likes it very gentle. She's very sensitive. It sounds like a music in my ears when she orgasms."

I blushed while Layla patted me on the leg.

"I'd like to hear that. I think you two should spend the night. Make music together. We can listen...listen to you play..."

Layla licked her fingers, feeling every one of Rico's wet kisses.

I leaned back down to the floor, next to Layla, who was getting very hot and bothered.

"Oh Savvy," she murmured, looking into

my eyes and falling in love.

"What?" I asked with a smile.

"Mmmm..." she groaned softly. "I want to kiss you."

I laughed weakly and continued staring into her pining eyes.

I leaned over closer, and planted a tender kiss on her lips.

"Mmmm...I liked that. You taste sweet."

I blushed and shook my hand in objection. "You're sweet for saying that."

"Huhh..." she exhaled deeply. "Touch me. I want to feel your touch against my skin. My skin's on fire right now...your skin cools me..."

"Mmmm!" she gasped shooting her intimate area up in the air bumping Rico a bit. I grabbed Layla's hand. We locked fingers and she squeezed me tightly.

"Oh God..." she sighed. "Hold my hand. Maybe you can feel what I feel. I pass the good vibes on to you."

"I need a lot more vibes to reach the point you're at, honey."

Layla tittered. "I might have the ones you're talking about—Ahhh!" she suddenly exclaimed. Oh, my pussy's so wet. It's so wet."

"I know. I can see it," I said, matching her eye contact and trying my best to connect with her.

"Ohh...my nipples...they're so hard..."

I looked down at her shaking nipples. I

hesitated for a moment, but then figured, what the hey, I might as well give her a little squeeze.

"Ohhh yeah!" she sung as I clutched her hard little nip and squeezed it lightly.

"Harder," she whispered.

I squeezed it a little bit harder and shook it around a bit, giving it a nice tug.

"Yeah...I like that. I like that."

I giggled and continued caressing Layla's firm but perfectly natural breasts.

"Is this turning you on, honey?" I asked Aaron.

"Oh yeah. Interactive porn is the best."

"What do you want to see me do?" I asked Aaron slyly.

"I dunno. Maybe sit on her face. Take both of our cocks inside of you."

I laughed loudly. "I'm afraid I'm not ready for that!"

"Oh, worth a shot."

"Ahaaa!" Layla said, reaching a climaxing point.

"Are you going to come?" I asked Layla moving my face in closer and invading her space.

"Yes!" she choked, writhing in ecstasy and convulsing all around me. "Oh God! I'm cumming! Oh Savvy, touch me! Touch me!"

I put my fingers her mouth and let her suck them, a preview of maybe naughtier things to come? My mistake though, she started cumming so hard she bit down on my index finger.

"Oww!"

She released her jaw lock and opened her mouth wide, letting that monster

orgasm out for all of us to enjoy. "Ohhhh God! Unhnnnn!"

She gasped and panted in the afterglow, holding her own breasts and smiling so

wide and free. "Mmm, that was a good one."

"So how do you feel?" Rico asked.

"That was very interesting," I said protectively. "I've never really heard another woman orgasm before, not in the same room, anyway."

"I've never heard you orgasm," Layla said playfully.

"No, I don't think I'm ready for that."

"Aww," Layla pouted. But it's so late. Why not go to sleep with us? We have a super king sized bed. "We can just lay around and see what happens."

"Mmm...I don't think so."

"Ohh, okay. I guess I won't keep bugging you about it. You're just so beautiful. I feel a certain spark," Layla assured me. "Between the two of us."

"And what about Aaron?"

"I like Aaron too. But usually the wives play first while the men watch."

"No complaints," Rico reminded. "I like a good show."

"Well, that's no fun. Wouldn't it be more fun if the guys could participate too?""Hmm, maybe," Layla said, thinking over her commandments and rules, which she probably seldom ever broke.

"Maybe you should think about it," I winked. "I think it would be really fun to see you out of your element for a change. A situation where you surrender control."

Layla stared at me a moment, appearing at once provoked and very interested. "Well, for you Savvy, maybe I would make an exception to the rule."

"Oh and by the way, honey?" I laughed totally disbelieving what I was about to do. You asked for proof I was a natural redhead?"

I raised my skirt revealing my little secret—no underwear and I was sporting a fully red carpet.

Layla's face lit up and she applauded, relieved to know the truth.

"Thank you, thank you."

"You went without panties the whole night?" Layla asked in shock. "To think my lips were so close to the promised land."

"Yes, so close. Actually...I didn't wear them to be sexy. I wore them because I was out of underwear. We need to do a wash!" I laughed at the absurdity of the moment.

Layla giggled, probably charmed and

equally annoyed at my conservative streak and my complete and unflappable resolve, to resist most of her whims. I never said scoring with me would be impossible. I just told her she would really have to work for it. Who knows what agonies or ecstasies I would demand from her? Only Aaron knows for sure and his lips are sealed. For now, my unveiling would be the subject of many of Layla's horny fantasies, until our inevitable next meeting. Since this was only the soft swap encounter...well, know who knows what the hard future may hold?

## 8 I WANT HIM

"Bitch," Judy muttered under her breath as she saw her neighbor reach up to get a can of tuna from one of the upper shelves. Norma Calendar. People have told Judy how irrational she sounded whenever she spoke of the woman who had made her life as miserable as she possibly could. But no one understood. She had hated Norma as soon as they met in elementary school.

Their relationship only became worse when they entered middle school where Norma made it a point to embarrass Judy every chance she could get. High school wasn't any better when she made sure to steal every guy Judy fell in love with just to spite her...just to win.

By the 1990s, Judy thought she could

finally put an end to this ridiculous and childish feud. It was the age of friendly sitcoms and political correctness. Judy offered to put the past behind them by inviting Norma and her vile husband over for coffee and doughnuts. "Great," she told herself then, thinking that they finally had a chance to outgrow the silly rivalry they had in their youth.

But it was a setup from the start, Judy realized, thinking back. Norma had used the opportunity to scout my new husband, trying to find holes in Judy's new marriage. She gritted her teeth as she remembered the way Norma shamelessly flirted with Matthew right in front of her and in front of Norma's husband. Matthew finally had sex with Norma and so Judy divorced his sorry ass.

But that didn't stop Norma from gloating her victory at every opportunity. She took an extended vacation with Matthew to Costa Rica and saw fit to write a very vulgar letter, bragging about stealing my husband and sending Judy pictures of their sexcapades and naked pictures of the man Judy thought would never betray her. Their relationship lasted for a few months before Norma left him. It wasn't surprising, really. She had only used Matthew as a way to spite Judy.

When they were both in their thirties, Judy had naively thought that maybe she could give friendship with Norma another try. She invited Norma over again, and the tramp pretended to be kind, at least for a while. Little did Judy know that Norma was still plotting, still trying to take one last thing from her.

At the time, Judy had been planning to adopt a child, and she told Norma how excited she was. The 3-year-old's name was Sean, and he was a regular playmate of Judy's biological son, Henry. When little Sean's mother died, Judy had felt responsible for him. For once in Judy's life, she felt whole. She felt she was going to do something life changing, for her and for Sean.

Judy wasn't surprised, deep down, when the adoption agencies turned her down because of claims of bad parenting and psychiatric problems. The agent had explained to her that they had received a call from an anonymous woman who told the adoption agency that Judy regularly participated in satanic cults and was a child beater.

Judy threw her cup of coffee in the sink, effectively breaking the china into pieces. Norma was a woman she tried very hard to love. But no matter how hard Judy tried, Norma wanted to make her life a living hell. Not only did Norma lie to the adoption agency, she had volunteered to adopt Sean herself! Norma, who could hardly hold down a relationship and was too barren and sterile to have children of her own, decided to adopt little Sean. She raised him and made it a point to send Judy a letter every week, gushing about how nice it was to have a child of her own and that Sean was a very well mannered boy.

Judy would be lying if she denied the fact that she was utterly obsessed with Norma Calendar's ultimate destruction. Even now, at their forties, Judy was still plotting to get back at Norma for all of the horrible things Judy had to endure because of her. And inspiration struck when Judy saw a post on one of those social networking sites where Norma wished her son a happy 18th birthday.

Norma had grown paranoid after years of tormenting Judy. So when Judy had commented on her post, she abruptly deleted it. Judy smiled as she refreshed her browser over and over again to find that Norma had, indeed, deleted the whole birthday post. She would have her vengeance soon.

The phone was ringing and Norma Calendar stopped reading the magazine in her hands to answer it. Her little boy was all grown up, and she was looking for the perfect gift ideas. She picked up the phone and put a smile on her face, a habit she had whenever she had to talk to someone on the phone.

"Hello?"

"Hi, Norma. It's Judy."

The smile on Norma's face quickly disappeared. She covered the mouthpiece with her other hand to give herself time to compose herself. The last time she and Judy had talked over the phone was years ago when she had invited Norma over and she found out about her wanting to adopt Sean. But that wasn't all that alarmed Norma. There was a cheery tone to Judy's voice that set Norma off. But she couldn't let Judy know that she was getting to her. But Judy already started talking before she could get a chance to reply.

"I just wanted to congratulate you," she said with the same cheery tone that made Norma clench her jaw. "After all, your son is finally...legal."

All thoughts of keeping calm flew out the window as she was reminded of her worst fear. "Fuck you, Judy," she spat, her nostrils flaring. "You stay away from—"

Click.

Judy had hung up on her and Norma was left staring at the phone in her hands. She gulped, hoping that she was just being overly paranoid and that Judy was just trying to scare her. But a little part of her knew that something untoward was going to happen.

Judy laughed loudly, the phone still in her hands. Norma's reaction had been priceless, and it made Judy incredibly excited to know that she was finally going to have her revenge. She walked up the stairs and into her bedroom with a smile on her face, wondering what she should wear tonight. Judy had no prior experience seducing someone who was barely a man; someone who was almost thirty years younger than her. But that only added to her thrill.

With Halloween on the way, things were only getting easier for Judy to plot her little scheme. She memorized Norma like the back of her hand, and she knew that Norma always went out to help the neighborhood kids go trick or treating during Halloween. Judy laughed, she definitely had a couple of tricks of her own, and Sean would definitely get a treat after all was said and done.

Come Halloween, Judy parked her car next to the red convertible in front of Norma's house. She walked up to the door and rang the bell, fixing her hair as she waited for Sean to answer the door. And when he did, his jaw dropped.

Sean could've sworn his jaw would hit the floor if it was capable of reaching that far. The woman in front of him was absolutely stunning. Her red hair fell to her waist in soft waves. She was wearing a red dress that showed off her voluptuous curves. She wore a matching red cape behind her back and matching red knee-high boots; and to top it off, she wore red horns on top of her head. Any other day, she probably would've been an eye sore, but today was Halloween and she fit right in. But what really caught Sean's eye were her big breasts. The dress was low enough that he could see plenty of cleavage even at a distance.

"Hi, you must be Sean," the woman said with a big smile on her face. She extended her hand in front of her. "My name's Judy, I'm a friend of your mother's."

Sean took her hand and shook it. "Nice to meet you, Judy. Yeah, I think I saw you last year at Mr. Wigg's funeral," he said. Judy still hadn't let go of his hand and was holding it rather tightly. Not that he minded, in fact, he was attracted to this woman. He could tell that she was in her forties, but she was still very attractive. "My mom isn't home, though. She went to help some of the kids trick or treat."

"Oh, is that right?" Judy replied, a pout setting on her face.

Sean sidestepped so that he could accommodate her. "You can wait here if you want. She'll probably be back in an hour."

She didn't hesitate and went inside the nicely decorated house. "What a gentleman," she said, smiling at him. "Norma raised such a fine young man. She must be proud." The words she used were all very kind, but Sean had a sense that there was a bit of sarcasm underneath her tone.

Without thinking more of it, he led her to the living room. "Do you want anything?" he asked her. "Coffee, soda, water...lemonade, maybe?" he finished with a smile that he knew charmed all the ladies.

She blushed like a teenager, just as Sean knew she would. But Judy was definitely not shy. She sat down on the couch, granting Sean a nice view of her cleavage. "Water would be great," she said, crossing her legs slowly.

"I'll be right back." Sean knew that the woman was trying to seduce him. He didn't mind, in fact, he was considering the idea of being seduced. He had just turned eighteen and the only females that he ever had sex with were mere girls. He had never experienced fucking someone older than him, even more so, someone who possibly could be as old as his mom.

Sean came back with two glasses of water. He put them down on the coffee table and sat down on the couch beside Judy, swinging his arm so it was resting on the backrest. 'Two can play this game," he thought to himself, smiling again at Judy.

"So, Judy," he said, tilting his head. "How long have you known my mother?" he asked. He had a feeling that his mom and this woman weren't actually friends.

"Oh, we've known each other since we were little girls," Judy replied, facing Sean and subtly jutting out her chest.

Sean didn't even bother concealing his fascination with Judy's breasts. Anyway, it seemed like this was really her intention. "Really?" he said, deliberately sounding distracted. "I see."

"Sean, dear," Judy said softly. "Didn't Norma ever tell you that it's rude to stare?"

The dark-haired 18-year-old pretended to snap out of his reverie and released a nervous laugh. "I'm so sorry. I didn't mean to stare. They're just really beautiful," he said, smiling cheekily. "I couldn't help wondering if they were..."

"Real?" Judy supplied, crossing her arms below her breasts, raising them a bit. "They're one hundred percent real, son. I was blessed, I guess," she finished, shrugging slightly.

"Hmm," Sean said, a frown settling on his face. "Mom always told me that all breasts that big are definitely fake."

Judy put on an indignant expression on her face. "Not mine!"

Sean shrugged. "I guess I'm just gonna have to take your word for it, Judy."

There was a moment where they didn't speak. It was as if they were calculating what would happen next. It was Judy who broke the silence.

"Well," she said, looking off to the sides. "You can touch them...if you want."

"Bingo," Sean thought, resisting the smile that was threatening to appear. If he knew that seducing cougars were so easy, he would've made it a point to chase them more. "Oh, I couldn't do that Judy," he said, putting his hands in front of him as if to prevent her from moving closer. "You're my mom's friend."

"It's quite alright, son," Judy replied, taking both of his hands and putting them on her partially covered breasts. "I want you to know that not all of what Norma says are true."

Sean caught the venom in her voice and figured that Judy must be using him to get back at his mother. But he couldn't care less as he started kneading the soft flesh beneath his hands. "I dunno..." he said, trailing off. He tilted his head as if to examine Judy's breasts. "I can't really tell if they're real with all this padding in your dress."

Judy raised an eyebrow. She had seen through his pretense at innocence and saw a spoiled, manipulative, and horny teenager. 'Two can play this game," she thought, smiling slightly as she started removing the straps of her red dress from her shoulders and unclasped the hooks on her strapless bra, letting her breasts hang free in front of her. She had nothing to be ashamed of, after all.

Sean's eyes widened at the sight of Judy's breasts in front of him. They were as real as Judy said they were, and they were beautiful. She truly was an attractive woman, even at her age. Without warning her, he leaned down and captured an unsuspecting nipple in his mouth, making Judy gasp but she made no move to stop him.

As Sean was pushing her gently down on the couch, Judy realized that she was so focused on seducing the young man that she had forgotten all about her little scheme. She had never expected that Sean would grow up to be a devilishly handsome man with a smile that could make even women her age blushing like a bunch of teenagers.

She reached down to lower the zipper of his jeans and felt that he was already hard. He felt enormous under her palm and she briefly wondered if she was right about the estimate of his size. Sean stopped sucking on her nipple to pull the shirt up and over his head, revealing his young taut body. He removed his jeans as well as the briefs that he was wearing, and Judy couldn't help but awe at the size of his cock. She had been right, his cock was huge.

Sean grinned at Judy's reaction as he revealed in her fascinated stare. She reached out to touch his cock, but he had other things in mind as he maneuvered himself so that he was directly under Judy's still-clothed pussy while she was facing his cock. Judy felt him pull down her panties so that her wet pussy was revealed to him. She knew exactly what Sean had in mind.

Judy leaned down, her pussy still in Sean's face, and rained licks and kisses on his cock before taking his entire length in her mouth. She sucked him noisily, making him groan at the back of his throat. Sean returned the favor and inserted his tongue in Judy's wet hole and fingered her clit. The vibrations from Judy's moans sent Sean reeling and he involuntarily bucked his hips.

Judy was no longer thinking of anything but enjoying this young man's hard cock. It was no surprise that both of them forgot the time. In the midst of pleasure, they had forgotten about Norma Calendar.

"In the name of—"

"In the name of—," Norma shouted, her shrill voice echoing through the house. She turned around and planned to walk away from the hideous sight when she remembered that this was her house and that was her son being defiled by the malicious Judy. "Get your crummy paws away from my son, Judy, or I'm calling the police!"

The redhead only laughed as she stood up from the couch and from Sean's naked body. He immediately used one of the throw pillows to cover himself. How could he have forgotten the time? Sean felt very stupid that moment.

"And tell them what?" Judy retorted, crossing her arms in front of her. "That I gave your 18-year-old son a blowjob? Oh, yes, Norma! I corrupted his perfectly legal mind," she finished with a laugh.

Norma had no answer for that, so she focused on Sean, who was quietly gathering his clothes on the floor. "Sean!"

she shouted at him, tears were already falling freely from her eyes. "How could you let this filthy woman into our home and do these unspeakable things with? How could you do this to me, your mother?"

"Mother?" Judy interrupted. "Norma, I can't believe you've been lying to Sean this entire time! We both know that Sean isn't really your son!"

Sean's eyes widened at Judy's words. He momentarily forgot his state of undress as he saw Norma's eyes widen with panic. "Wait," he said, putting a hand to his temple. "Mom, what is Judy talking about?"

"Yeah, Norma," Judy said, looking at Norma triumphantly as she sat down on the couch. "What am I talking about?"

Norma sighed. She had hoped that this day would never come. Or if it did, that Sean didn't have to find out this way. "Sean, baby," she started to say as she walked towards him "You're adopted."

"You're adopted."

Sean stepped away from the woman he thought was his mother all these years. His mind was reeling from the events that were taking place.

"She adopted you to spite me!" Judy

screamed, standing up suddenly, her eyes wide with anger. "I was going to be Sean's mother, and you stole him away from me!"

"Enough!" Sean shouted. He looked at the both of them, rage and betrayal etched on his face. He let the throw pillow fall to the floor as he walked to Norma and took both her hands in his. He forced her to sit down on one of the wooden chairs. Without letting go of her hands, he picked his leather belt from the ground and tied them behind Norma's back. He walked to Judy and ripped the red cape and her panties from her. He used the cape to tie Norma's feet together.

"What are you doi—," Norma started to say, when Sean put Judy's panties in her mouth, effectively stopping her from talking.

"You used me!" Sean shouted at her. "I'm not some object you can use for your own sick pleasure!"

Judy watched this calmly with her arms crossed in front of her when Sean faced her and pushed her quite roughly on the couch. "And you!" he shouted at her, his hand cupping her chin forcefully. "You're just like her! You used me to get back at her!"

He held Judy's red dress in his hands and a resounding rip rang through the house. "I'm going to teach both of you a lesson!" He looked back at Norma who was looking at him fearfully. "Don't look away, mother. This show is just for you," he said, his voice dripping with venom as he thrust into Judy's willing pussy. Judy let out a surprised gasp as he plunged into her again and again. She turned her head to glance at Norma when Sean slapped her strongly across the face. Tears fell from her eyes as she looked up at him.

"You wanted to be my mother, didn't you Judy?" he asked as he gripped her thighs rather painfully. "You wanted to be my mother but you sucked my cock and you let me eat your pussy! You're just as sick as she is!" He withdrew his cock from her and pulled on Judy's red hair. Judy yelped in pain as she was forced to walk naked towards Norma. Sean put her hands on either side of Norma's head before plunging back into her from behind. Judy's breasts were painfully close to Norma's face that Norma turned her head sideways.

"I told you not to look away!" Sean shouted as he slammed inside Judy so hard that she stumbled right into Norma as her arms went around her neck. As much as the situation pained her, Judy felt unbelievable pleasure course through her body. It was an exhilarating feeling to be fucked and humiliated this way that she didn't mind Sean's hard slaps on her butt cheeks as he fucked her again and again.

Judy came with a shout, her knees shaking beneath her. Sean pulled on her hair again. "I'm not done yet!" he screamed at her as he pounded into her again and again. He came after ten more thrusts, withdrawing his cock so that his semen would fly straight into Norma's face. She was sobbing when he finished. Sean let Judy fall to the floor.

He sat down on the couch as he stared at the two women in front of him. "So..." he said, an evil smile forming on his lips. "Shall we make peace over a group shower?"

# 9 THE TRIFECTA: LOVING THREE GENERATIONS

My name is Don John, and yes, I pattern my life after the Don Juan of literary works, the libertine who was a lover of women, a connoisseur of the female anatomy, embracing it in all ages and stations of life. I am a violent man, a gambling man, and a ruthless man. My only weakness is my desire, my yearning to sample the pleasures of every woman I meet.

To me, life is a journey and there are many roads of discovery. A road less traveled is a lonely road. Therefore, I choose not to limit myself to one woman, or to discriminate against certain types of women. To do so would be to deny the libertine lifestyle, to and limit the value of physical pleasures.

Some of the most passionate affairs I have ever had have been with women perceived to be "less" than the norm.

In my first year traveling around the United Kingdom, I made it a point to sample the pleasures of a woman from every decade. The younger women whose treasures I enjoyed, I found to be vibrant, experimental and effervescent. The older women I found not only challenging but also invigorating; their levels of experience introduced me to new peaks, new epiphanies of the human body.

When I traveled outside my own comfortable soil, I made it a point to make peace with my racist ancestry; throughout the course of a year, I made love to a woman of every race and ethnicity. I discovered that each woman I loved was a self-contained country. She contained years of culture, of warring and of reconciliation in her vagina. To cross a woman, to betray her heart, would be to start a generational war.

My greatest goal was to travel to the Americas, a melting pot of diversity, of excess and of ambition. To have sex with an American woman was not only an honor but a burden; a challenge and a threat only the bravest lovers would accept.

My first goal upon earning my visa was

to make love to as many chubby beauties as possible. I found big, beautiful women to be not only eager to please, but also quite curvy and thus able to pleasure me in unique ways that skinny women could not do.

Whenever young men would ask me, How & Why, I would reply that "Honesty is the only aphrodisiac. When one loses sight of his honesty, he has lost his way and does not deserve the love of a woman."

However, the greatest feat of all, my unbridled and dream ambition, was the trifecta; three generations of the same female personality. I had already made love to mothers, to barely legal Lolitas, and to libidinous seniors—but to possess three women of the same family was to look God in the eye and spit in her pussy.

What made the challenge so inviting was not just the love, the conquering, but also the threat of death. For threatening a woman in this manner, to expose her frailties, and challenge her to accept her own mortality and weakness, was to summon up a demon of jealousy. The very thought of being murdered by three angry women of the same bloodline was arousing to me. What better way to die than be killed by three related vaginas of hate?

The seduction was easy. I chose the mother first. Single mothers have always been proverbially lonely and quick to idealize a strong male figure in their lives. While they long to provide a healthy upbringing for their children, they are robbed of sensual pleasure at night, and must reconcile a dual issue of indulgence and restraint. The promise of commitment is what attracts them and unleashes their angry, hungry passion.

April was beautiful. What I found most appealing about her was her lonely and kind disposition, her expressive and silly eyes and her shy smile. She dyed her hair black, perhaps as a warning to the men that hoped to conquer her; as if to say, I am no pushover but a challenge. In the beginning, she resisted me. She thought my charms to be misplaced. It was only after perseverance and painting the illusion of dependence that she finally caved to her desires.

I still remember her face the night she agreed to accompany me to dinner. Her face, once so cold and distant, was now warm and rekindled with interest. She waited upon my every word and desired to know what was resonating inside my mind.

She prettied herself up, wearing a light green dress, quite formal, with only a hint of sex appeal. It was endearing that she wanted to save the best of her gifts for a more secluded, safe environment. She desired my trust and hid her body like a deck of cards. Waiting for me ante up, she asked me such deep and personal questions, designed to expose my deviant plot.

I answered her in kind, piquing her mind, and creating a whirlwind of ideals, a mirage to build a dream life on.

April's mother Kathy was not an easy affair to forge. She did not know of my relationship with April, the younger mother, but did sense that I was unwholesomely interested in her. I pride myself on being ageless, on having a timeless face that could captivate any audience. Still, she felt that I was her inferior, being a "younger man" who desired a cougar's bite.

I assured Kathy that age was merely a number and made it a point to prove my intellectual superiority—a challenge she found provocative and yet very alluring. A young man who had achieved so much wisdom at an early age was truly worth her attention. Perhaps he was destined to be great; perhaps she would be the strong woman who would tame the beast.

Kathy took a while to come around, but when she did, her tranquil eyes and courageous smile—taking a chance on love—was inspiring to me. The first time she agreed to accompany me to a theme park, it was joy to behold her face, a once stone cold rock mass, dissolving into a human face.

Even though she was in her early fifties, she took great pride in her fit body. She wore short shorts and a tight blouse for our first non-date, so that she could accentuate her breasts and thin waist. Her spunky, spiked golden hair charmed me. She was determined to prove to me and the world that despite her age, she had no intention of slowing down.

The last woman on my hit list was Jasmine, the youngest of the matriarch. An eighteen-year-old girl, with red-dyed hair, and as spiteful a beast as any woman I had ever met. She was the easiest lay, quite frankly, as young daughters are naturally attracted to the men who date their mothers. It revitalizes the competition and challenges a foolish girl's ambitions.

Jasmine knew that I was dating her mother April. April had two children, the first Jasmine, now living on her own, and the second one Jordan, a boy still dependent on his mother. Despite the affair blossoming, Jasmine's thirst for dramatic encounters and secret liaisons was too great for either she or I to resist.

The first time we met, we met in her house. I remember her naughty little face welcoming me inside. She would gutturally laugh at every observation I made, showing herself to be in heat, in lust and in denial of our moral corruption.

Her bob haircut was adorable, and her fashion sense was the most sophisticated of the three women; probably because she was the most undecided, the boldest and the least tied down. She kept her options and her legs open to the world. I don't recall much about the brown evening dress she wore to our first meet up, but I distinctly remember her lifting her skirt and imparting to me a grand revelation; that she neglected to wear panties, in expectation of our illicit affair.

When April was ready, I made sure to leave the lights on shining brightly because I wanted to see every detail of her flawed but fantastic naked body. She let me undress her. I wanted her to wait still, staring only into my eyes, while I stripped her of her dignity. Her children thankfully out of the way, her mother parts were all mine for the plundering.

I always go for the breasts first, especially in mothers, as I want evidence as to their maternal comforts. Every woman in this family had large D cup breasts; it was the one inheritable trait I observed. April wore a full support bra because of her active lifestyle. Removing it was such a treat, since it was such an elaborate production.

When her breasts escaped their prisons, I couldn't help but suckle and fondle them, even while we both stood in her bedroom. I lost track of time and space and kissed her pointy nipples for what seemed like hours. She giggled at my obsession and felt it necessary to lead me to the bedroom for a more relaxing rendezvous.

She lay on the bed and invited me to suckle on her breasts once again. I jumped on the bed and attacked her once forbidden fruits with rage and violence. I sucked her nipples hard and made sure to pinch the spare when my mouth was in pursuit. Her cautious words to slow down was like music to my ears.

"Wait," she laughed, pushing my head away. "My nipples are sensitive."

"Then maybe it's time to put my burning tongue to better use."

I clasped her breasts with my eager hands as I lowered myself down to her white, glistening panties. I smelt her essence through the material, longing to taste her watery garden. I could tell she had reservations about dirty sex, as she tried to dissuade me from tasting her. But I was possessed by a demon of love. I kissed her mound through her panties enticing her, daring her to stop me.

She sighed and nervously prepared for a messy ride. I wanted her to give me her mess. I wanted to flood my mouth with her bodily secretions.

My angry tongue would wait no longer. I gently pulled her panties off but had not the patience to pull them off from her legs. Her panties only halfway down to her hips I began loving her precious button, her clitoris which was shy at first, but which warmed up to me the more I called for it.

"Oh...that feels so good," she sighed but with more reservations. "I don't know if I'm ready."

"Ready to experience divine pleasure?"

"I haven't...lost control in so long."

"Surrender yourself," I said before I intensified my lashing.

"Ohhh! It feels so good..."

"Don't hold back. Give me more of your sweet, beautiful pussy."

She groaned and did as I asked, spreading her legs farther apart, so that I could sink my tongue deep into her wet caverns.

"It's too much!" she cried.

"Surrender."

I ate her beautiful slosh while rubbing

her hot spot with fervor. If she was going to come, I wanted it to exude, to erupt on my face.

"Oh! Oh John!" she screamed, quaking with ecstasy and humping my face.

She exhaled profoundly as the room seemed to spin. "Oh yeah, oh yeah," the single mom gasped, as I continued to stay buried in her vaginal treasures, admiring the artistry of her stretch marks. Her every mole, freckle and wrinkle was a victory, and he sought comfort in her bushy little treasure map for long moments even after her glorious orgasm.

"I want to suck you," April aggressively said to me, eager to give me the same pain and pleasure I subjected her to.

"Slow down, my love. I don't know if I can take it..."

"Oh you're going to take it," fondling my naked body and kissing her way to my midsection.

"Yes..." I suspired. "Kiss me; extinguish the fire in my soul."

She stroked my hard tool, preparing me for agony, and grabbed some pre-cum for a juicier squeeze. I sighed in patience, but was quickly losing my resolve. The moment she swallowed me with her desperate, lonely lips I almost lost my wits. She sucked me with cruelty, plundering my man oil and staring at me in haughty vengeance. She dared me to lose control; she dared me to leave her. She sucked me in, and had no intention of ever letting go.

I pushed back against her face in a moment of weakness, which only provoked her to sink deeper into depravity. She released my manhood and then sentenced her gobbling claws to my testicles.

"Yeah...you want me to suck your balls?"

"Yes," I exclaimed, ashamed of my volume.

"Yeah?" she said licking my delicate sack and then swallowing up my family jewels.

"What do you want?" she asked in total surrender, as if to negotiate a permanent price.

"Mmm...go lower," I said.

"Lower?"

She hesitated a moment but strengthened her resolve, wanting to win the bid and prove herself a true libertine. As she filled my anus with her wiggling tongue, I knew the kind of whore April was; a devoted one, a kept woman who would sacrifice all of her ideals for the perfect fantasy.

"Where do you want me to unleash myself?" I asked, feeling the fire in my loins.

"Inside of me."

Of course she did, perhaps to ensure

another pregnancy, or to accustom me to the warm, protective home she thought I desired.

"Cum in me, John! I want to feel your cum!"

When I ejaculated inside of her, she clutched me tight with her vaginal walls, and shook the entire region making sure I orgasmed in inhibition.

Even when we were finished love making, she continued to fondle and play with my penis, like it were a most precious gem.

"Did you like it?" she asked in neediness.

When I succeeded in my quest to taste Kathy's drying fruits, we were both so consumed with fire; we opted not to wait until the home journey. Instead, we checked into a random hotel, made up fake names and paid cash. As soon as we entered the empty room, I shoved her on the bed and let my ugly passion overtake us both.

Yes, my rage was alarming and beastly. But having been sex deprived and trust deprived for so long, Kathy let me defile her—she encouraged my misbehavior and tore open her own blouse hastily, desiring nothing more than to feel my hot kisses and vicious tongue on her intimacy.

I ripped this grandma's blouse apart, plundering her temple, wanting to reduce her aging grace to a puddle of whore stench. I ripped every shred of protection she had until I found a most pleasing sight: she wore a minimizing bra, which protected her giant pillows from the detection of young and virile men. Perhaps she was ashamed or afraid of what wolves might linger, yearning to taste her fleshy parts. She could not hide from me.

I detested her green brassiere and ripped it from her body, scavenging for her mature breasts, which were bouncing away from me in terror. When I did find her nipples I attacked—to which she responded with a delightful scream.

Age meant nothing; a body was a body and I sucked and bit her nipples without discrimination. She appreciated my lack of respect and brought me closer to her bosom to ravage her.

She pushed me upwards so she could unfasten my pants and feel my hardened spirit. To her surprise and joy, there was nothing between her and I but a thin layer of pants. She touched my swinging dagger and kissed it tenderly under the head, enjoying my quivering reaction.

She grouped her breasts together and welcomed my erection into her bountiful baskets. Her breast pillows hugged me tightly and defied me to escape. I repeatedly stabbed her with my throbbing sword reducing her to slag meat.

"Let me taste you," I demanded, desiring to taste her wine-like vulva juice, and compare the subtle flavor differences between mom and daughter.

She lifted her skirt and dropped her granny panties allowing me to behold her thin bush and open valley. Her stretch marks were even more pronounced but they only added character to her vagina's unique face.

Her flavors were very similar to April's—they both tasted like red wine, and when they gushed out to me, they flooded my face with herbal delights.

I licked Kathy's magic button with unbridled excitement, loving the very idea of stealing an older woman's treasures. As I felt her wet carpet sponging my forehead, I noticed her vagina contracting, an imminent orgasm approaching.

I stuck my fingers inside and searched for her heavenly bean, her hidden switch that would activate her full throttle mode and send the old crow into orgasmic bliss.

"Oh right there!" Kathy screamed. "Oh my god…"

"What's the matter?" I said, pounding her Great Spot, and holding my hand on her pubic mound.

"It's never felt this good…hmmm!" She

panted nervously. "I'm usually so quiet..." she giggled in discomfort. "B-But this is different."

"Hold nothing back. I want to see you get dirty, Kathy."

"Oh God!" she screamed gyrating and contorting her pelvis, but unable to escape my locking grip.

"Oh God Oh God Oh God!" she screamed. "I think I'm going to pee!"

Her entire frame rattled and she tried her best to hold the waters back. "Oh John! I'm cumming so hard!" But nothing could prevent her from squirting all over my face, a delightful combination of cum and piss. Like aged vinegar, I licked it up without regret or hesitation.

"Oh Jesus," Kathy said, grabbing her heart and backing away from me— escaping the wild animal who was destroying her will.

She felt self-conscious and hid her aging body from me, covering her vulnerable snatch, and reaching for a pillow.

"Don't be afraid," I assured her. "Lose yourself to me. It's all I want, Kathy. For us both to reach new levels of ecstasy."

She laughed. "You talk so funny sometimes, John. But I guess all you Europeans do. Tell me Don John...what do you like women to do to you?"

"Whatever their uninhibited heart

desires. Whatever is too safe, I despise."

"I know what I want. But is it what you want?"

"I could guess," I said slyly, and I did guess long before she asked.

"I want you to cum in my pussy."

Of course, they all do, or at least the women in this family.

"I want nothing more than to fill you up with my seed."

"Don't worry...I'm fixed. No unexpected pregnancies."

"How unfortunate. Impregnating such a beautiful woman is every boy's wet dream.

She laughed and grabbed me by the hair, forcing me to stuff her cavern full of manly glory.

"Talk to me," she insisted.

"What shall I say, my love?"

"No talk to me dirty."

"Dirty? You like to be violated? Humiliated?"

"Yeah...yeah...I do!" she said, as she complemented by thrusts with deep pushes and pulls, creating double the friction for my loaded weapon.

"Then tell me what a whore you are, Kathy."

"Oh yeah! Fuck me! Fuck me John! Cum inside of me! I want you to creampie me, you big young stud."

I do adore when women do the dirty talking for me, it saves me the effort and allows the slattern to earn her pay.

Kathy's vagina squeezed me tightly just as April's once did. It is definitely a family trait, and one that I look forward to sampling at least one more time in the near future. When I ejaculated deep in Kathy's cataclysmic hole, I appreciated how she used her hands—clinging to me, worshiping me, and fondling me, a chorus of applause.

Her smoldering, creamy box didn't let me go, and so I enjoyed my dick sauna for a few quiet moments. She stroked my head, as if begging me not to leave her, to fill the void once and forever.

Jasmine wanted to make love solely as a way of acting out against her mother, whom she suspected I was romancing. Stealing her young but not quite virginal body was an easy feat. When they are young as dear Jasmine, a man's words are like axes and each and every look he gives is a call to attention.

When Jasmine closed the door behind us, I didn't feel the need to tear her clothes off. Instead, I wanted her to unveil herself for me. To dance and to present herself for my celebration.

She took the idea in kind and shoved me on the couch so that I could get a heavenly strip show. She removed one article of clothing at a time, selling herself like a professional, and smiling wide at me, begging for fatherly attention.

"Come on. Be sexier," I commanded.

She sent me a cold shoulder at first, but then danced twice as hard and slutty, as she was determined to prove her youthful superiority over the two cougars.

She took off her party dress and treated me to a most wonderful site: a cup-less bra, with a brassiere frame, but with no support cups. Instead, her exposed nipples protruded out, inviting me to tinker with them. Like her mother and her grandmother, Jasmine's breasts were enormous and could hardly manage without a bra, but for times as celebratory as this, unencumbered flesh was all that mattered.

She sat on the couch, straddling me, and shoved her mammaries in my face, jiggling them without a worry or a second thought. She was indeed the tigress when compared to her aging, insecure mothers. Perhaps the burden of motherhood is what robs a woman of her confidence. Jasmine welcomed sex and basked in its glow.

When I suggested we move into the bedroom, I was sold on this trollop and desired to disgrace her even more than the others.

First things first—I demanded to taste

her creamy pie, just to see if age made her unique taste slightly pungent or sweeter than her predecessors. This newest model was a treat all right; her pussy lips were spicy and her wetness tasted almost sugary. It is possible she flavor-douched herself prior to our affair, she being the most modern world conscious of three generations.

Like her mother and her grandmother, Jasmine was a loud screamer and nothing brought her to orgasm faster than a quick lick job. I signed my name in cursive and had her exploding all over the bed and all over my face.

"Oh John! Fuck! You're going to make me cum baby! Ohhhh!" she groaned and bounced her thighs all over my ears, having sat her snatch upon my head.

She had a bit of a cloying gasp, self-indulgent and not nearly as sophisticated as Kathy's or as proud as April's. Still, I found her scent lovely and her internal temperature smoldering.

"Now you," she demanded. "I want to make you cum just as loud."

"I don't know if that's possible."

"You cocky bastard! What, do you think younger women are trash or something? Just because you fucked my mother?"

And her grandmother.

"I don't know what you're talking about."

"Oh bullshit," the wise one said. "Don't pretend as if I'm some stupid little girl who doesn't see through your bullshit act. Maybe mom buys it, but not me. I just wanted to fuck you to teach mom a lesson."

How dare she question my honesty, I thought to myself. And suddenly, I did desire her, despite her cloying voice and baby-like mannerisms. I wanted to corrupt her in unspeakable ways, the likes of which she would never feel again.

I grabbed her in dominance and tossed her to the bed on her back.

"Yeah! Fuck me like you mean it!"

I shoved my hand in her mouth as I filled her spiteful little pussy with rage. I thrust my erection deep inside of her, slamming into her cervix and pounding her precious little chastity box with a pirate's strength.

"Is that all you got?" she taunted me.

I fucked the little bitch even harder, even while she taunted me and chopped down my respect of her.

"Oh yeah!" she screamed, writhing with me and making our connection even tighter and wetter.

Just as I felt the urge to strike escape from her, she used the family secret weapon and tightened her pelvic muscles, rendering my penis helpless.

"Do you like that, John? Is that how

you fuck my mom too? Do our pussies feel the same to you?"

"Shut up," I muttered as I withdrew my sword.

"What's the matter? Too nasty? You're the one doing it..."

"I'll show you nasty, you little tart."

I took my manhood in hand and shoved it into her mouth, making the brat taste her own creamy filling.

She took it in her out mouth and spit it out. "Oh yeah! Do it, nasty boy!"

She licked and sucked her own pussy off and looked exactly as I imagined her.

"Fuck me again! I want to taste myself!"

The most depraved of three generations taunted me to keep up the assault, and defile her in a way that perhaps I could not even fathom. To finish the child, I crawled on top of her and lifted her bulbous backside into the air, and found her tight little o-ring. I plunged my meat into that dormant volcano top and listened for her mad objection.

She had no such warnings, but continued to taunt me, the insatiable giant, she was. "Oh yeah! Fuck my asshole, you dirty boy! You like fucking moms and daughters up the ass?"

"Only yours, you little demon."

"Yeah, fuck it! Oh God yeah! Make my asshole cum!"

Wouldn't you know the mad little one

did have an ass of fire and had the most peculiar of abilities. She tightened her anal sphincter muscles and gripped my manhood ruthlessly even in the most peculiar of places. Her tight hole hugged me as her arching body taunted not to explode at the most inappropriate time.

No, this was not defilement enough. She dared to dance with the devil and now had to reap the tricklings of Hell.

I pulled out my throbbing penis and shoved it into her mouth, silencing her with the taste of her own feedback.

"Mmmph!" she screamed as I abused her mouth and rammed my pole into the Gag-Spot.

I withdrew and listened to her gasping and choking like a symphony.

I wasn't even going to ask her the ultimate question, because I already knew this family in very intimate ways.

I threw her back down to her back and inserted myself into her warm, wet treasure box—so much like her mother and grandmother in texture and temperature, it almost made me laugh.

"Ohhhh yeah! Cum inside me!"

I grunted and gritted as I exploded inside of her, reserving the heaviest burden for the most ungrateful of the bunch.

I turned to my side and panted to catch my breath.

She crawled on top of me and eyed me dangerously—like a tigress on the hunt.

"I can't believe you went through with it. You tell my mother you love her and then fuck her daughter?"

I said nothing but inhaled slowly.

"So tell me. Who did you like better? Whose pussy was the best? Or do we both feel the same to you?"

"There are similarities. But subtle differences," I shrugged.

"Uh huh. So answer the question. Who do you prefer?" She said, holding an invisible gun and daring me to make a move.

"You were the tightest squeeze, Jasmine."

"Uh huh," she said suspiciously.

"Your mom was the most adventurous and the best feeling."

"Really?"

"But..." I grinned devilishly. "Your grandmother's pussy tasted the best."

She backed away from me and dropped her jaw in amazement. "Oh my God! You...you had sex with all three of us? You mean...grandma's talking about you? You're the new guy in her life?"

"Is there a problem?"

"You're insane!" She hopped out of bed and frantically looked for her clothes.

"Don't even ask me to keep this a secret. We're coming back for you. You have to answer for this."

"That's fine."

"To think that poor grandma finally thought she found the one."

"She did find the one. However, The One is not always what we long him to be."

"Darling," I said, a bit worried. "Are you going to tell your mother and grandmother that I penetrated your most precious of holes?"

"You know what? I think I will. Because I hate you and my mother equally."

"Good," I replied, smiling in relief.

I always said that honesty was the only weapon I needed to live as Don John, the reincarnation of Don Juan, a true spirit that time has erased and renamed as fiction. In my arrogant quest to possess the trifecta, I displaced my honesty, and became three different men just to appease three lonely women. Perhaps it was an unforgiveable sin. Not that knowing three blood-related vaginas was in itself a transgression; but taking such a spurious short may been my felo de se.

By the time I attempted to return to an honest lifestyle, by telling Jasmine what she wanted to know, and what she did not know, too much damage had already been done. I could not repair the tower of lies I had impacted. All that remained was the tumble down to humility, the king's mighty fall.

And so I wait, not for reconciliation, not for forgiveness but to die. For I know that like Don Juan, I will meet a violent end and the hands of three scorned women. I will try my best to romance three hearts simultaneously, if not to keep them in my possession, than at least to plead for my life.

I know the ending. All that is left is to die. To die a lover's death. Passion in life, passion in the bedroom, and passion the moment you expire.

But what a way to die, surrounded by three women whose vaginas I can still taste upon my lips.

They're here. They have brought weapons. I do suppose this will be my final diary entry. God have mercy on me in Hell.

# 10 ACCIDENTAL SEX

## Prologue

It was five am in the morning when Danielle heard the horrendous ringing of the telephone that wouldn't stop no matter how long she ignored it. It would stop ringing for a while, only to start again after a few minutes. She groaned loudly and reached to her left where her husband Ben was still talking in his sleep.

Danielle, with her eyes still closed, started tapping whatever body part she could reach to wake him up because the phone was on his bedside table. When that didn't work, she started shaking what felt to be his thigh.

'Yes!' she shouted mentally to herself triumphantly when she felt him move, only to realize that Ben only shifted his position so that he was facing away from her. She sighed angrily, opened her eyes, sat up, reached over, and picked up the phone.

"What?" she shouted into the mouthpiece. "Do you realize how goddamn early it—"

"Good moooorning, sleepyhead!" came the cheerful reply from the other end, interrupting Danielle from her angry tirade. The voice was female, chipper, and sounded all too familiar.

Danielle moaned, not bothering to conceal how annoyed she felt. "Sarah, it's 5'oclock in the fucking morning. What the hell do you want?"

"Don't you know what day it is?"

It was then that Danielle remembered, snapping out of her reverie. "Shit."

There was a chuckle on the other end. "That's right! We're going to the Bahamas!"

## At First Sight

Sarah had been waiting for this trip for months and now, they were finally going to the Bahamas! It would be like going out on a double date. Except that this double date was going to last five days. Not to mention that it was probably going to be the best vacation ever! The Bahamas! Woohoo!

This was what Sarah was thinking as

she and Victor, her husband, waited for her friend and her husband to come out of their house. She reached over to the steering wheel and slammed the horn twice for the third time. "Come on guys!" Sarah shouted, grinning ecstatically. "We don't wanna miss our flight!"

"Honey, don't rush them," Victor said, stifling a yawn with his hand. "People tend to forget something important when you rush them like that."

Sarah ignored her husband like she did most of the time, but settled down in her seat. She was just so excited. She hadn't seen her good friend Danielle in years, and she had yet to meet her husband Ben. All this excitement was killing her and she was having a hard time containing it.

It was less than a minute later when Danielle and Ben finally came out of the house with their luggage. Ben was the first to come out and Sarah couldn't help but notice how handsome he looked and how hot his body was. His navy blue shirt was tight enough on his body that she could make out his washboard abs. He had a boyish charm to him with his wavy brown hair that seemed a bit too long. Sarah decided that he and Danielle were a perfect match when she saw her blonde friend looking stunning in a short flowery dress that accentuated her delicious curves and showed off her tan legs.

"That's Danielle?" Victor asked. Sarah didn't miss the awe in his voice and turned to look at him. Sure enough, he was staring at Danielle. She felt a little jealous and wished she had worn a dress as well. But without Danielle's voluptuous curves and big breasts, she doubted she stood a chance.

She rolled her eyes and stepped out of the car, waving at the good-looking couple. Any sign of irritation was gone, replaced with a smile. "Oh my god, Danielle! How long has it been?" she said, wrapping her arms around Danielle who didn't hesitate hugging her back.

"Too long, that's for sure," the blonde replied with a chuckle. "Let me introduce to you my husband. This is Ben. Ben this is Sarah."

Sarah shook Ben's outreached hand and looked up at him. He looked even more handsome up close. This guy was a hunk, and he didn't bother being modest about it. She could feel his eyes boring into her even though he was wearing mirrored sunglasses and it ran a chill up her spine. "Hi," she said nervously and berated herself for being so obvious.

Ben grinned at Sarah, amused at her reaction and her apparent attraction to him. He felt the same way, of course. The brunette in front of him looked like a model with her white tank top and denim shorts. She didn't have his wife's D-cup sized breasts, but what she did have, that Ben wished Danielle had as well, were slim, creamy legs that seemed to go on and on forever. But what really made an impact on him were Sarah's bright green eyes that were looking shyly up at him.

Only about a second passed before Ben and Sarah let go of each other's hands. The interaction between them happened so quickly that Danielle didn't even notice it happening. Or maybe it was because she was too busy noticing Victor's husky voice that made her bite the corners of her lips, or how broad his shoulders were.

But she and Sarah seemed to have the same thought in mind.

This is gonna be a long vacation...

## A Long, Long Drive

Victor was a somewhat serious man. He always woke up at five am in the morning, even without an annoying clock to wake him up. He'd put on a pair of sweatpants, a tee, running shoes, and jogged around the neighborhood for a good two hours before coming home to a delicious breakfast at seven am. It'd take exactly thirty minutes to finish his food with Sarah, and then he'd take a ten to fifteen-minute shower. He put on his clothes and fixed his short red hair quickly that by eight o'clock, he was done and ready to go to work.

Life was routine for Victor. While some people might be opposed to the idea of having that kind of lifestyle, Victor reveled in it. That didn't mean he was boring. It just meant that he was...a somewhat serious man.

And his encounter with Danielle knocked him off routine. He definitely did not expect her to be as beautiful as she was. He could've sworn his cock twitched at the sight of her. It wasn't that he didn't love his wife or that he didn't find her attractive. He did, and Sarah was as beautiful as they come. Tall, slender, and graceful...he was a lucky bloke to have her.

But Danielle with her long blonde hair, curvy physique, and big breasts was a sight to behold. Up close, she looked like an angel. She had these big hazel eyes you could stare at all day and drown in and she smelled sweet like vanilla. When they shook hands earlier, and he touched her skin for the first time, electricity had run through his entire body. He knew, then, that he was attracted to her.

Images of Danielle entered his mind, and he desperately tried to will them away, knowing that if it continued, he would have a hard-on that he wouldn't be able to explain to Sarah. Victor had only been driving for a couple of minutes and it'd be another hour before they reached the airport and he didn't want to walk around sporting a big boner. He succeeded in vanquishing all of the erotic thoughts from his brain except for the image of his cock sliding in between the blonde's large breasts with her tongue darting out to lick the tip. It was something he had never been able to do with his wife with her average-sized breasts.

It didn't help that whenever he had to look at the rear-view mirror, Danielle always seemed to be looking at him. She only looked away when he would catch her, but sometimes they would make eye contact, only breaking it when Victor had to go back to looking at the road. He wasn't oblivious. He knew when someone was attracted to him, and Danielle was definitely attracted.

Shit. Victor was going to have to stop thinking about the blonde beauty behind him or else he really was going to have an erection jutting from his pants. He sighed. This was going to be a long, long drive.

### The Bahamas

They arrived at the hotel after four hours of sitting on the plane with an awkward silence looming over them. The only person who seemed oblivious to it all was Ben, who chatted animatedly with anyone who would listen to him. He talked with Danielle and Sarah mainly about the things that they would do once they landed. Victor was mostly silent, which was normal for him. There was plenty of tension and the flight was long enough for them to take a nap, but nobody really need.

Sarah couldn't sleep, for some reason. Maybe it was because Ben kept stealing glances at her. He wouldn't stop even during the times when Sarah would catch him staring. He'd just give her this toothy grin that made her heart beat faster. She was starting to think that maybe she shouldn't have planned this trip at all. Little did Sarah know, Victor and Danielle were thinking the same thing. Ben seemed to be the only person on this trip who was glad to be there.

It was when they landed that all of the tension disappeared, only to be replaced by sheer excitement. By the time they got into the van that would take them to the hotel, they were all talking and the vehicle was filled with ooohs and aaahs as they took in the paradise that was the Bahamas.

Sarah planned the whole trip from where they would stay for five days to the bunch of activities they could indulge in and when they walked into the hotel and drank in the sight of the beautiful interior, she knew she had made the right choice.

Danielle was the first to break out of the trance. "Sarah, you're a genius!" she exclaimed.

"Yeah, honey, this hotel looks amazing," Victor said, unable to take his eyes off the magnificent sight in front of them.

"Yeah, beautiful," Ben suddenly said. Sarah looked at him, but Ben wasn't looking at the hotel. No, the dark-eyed man was looking at her intently. There was no smile on his face. He was just staring at her. "Absolutely breath-taking."

Sarah looked away, unable to maintain eye contact any longer. She knew she had turned into a shade of red that could've rivaled that of a tomato.

They were greeted by two cheerful hostesses who lead them to the front desk. Sarah had booked a two-bedroom suite on one of the upper floors months ago, thinking that it would be a good set-up for the two couples to get to know one another. Now, she was starting to regret her decision.

When they reached their suite, Sarah momentarily forgot the awkwardness of the situation. She and Danielle ran around the room, gushing about the beautiful furniture and the even more beautiful view of the beach from the balcony as the men set down their luggage. Ben went over to the fridge, got out a bottle of wine, poured the red liquid inside four crystal champagne flutes, and offered them to his three companions.

"To Sarah," Ben said, tipping his glass in a toast. "For planning out the best vacation we'll ever have."

"Here, here," Victor quipped.

"Cheers," Danielle said, clinking her glass with Sarah's as the green-eyed beauty blushed for the umpteenth time that day.

But none of them knew just what this trip had in store for them.

## Over A Bowl Of Cereal

That night, Danielle couldn't sleep. It wasn't that the bed was uncomfortable. In fact, it was the exact opposite. As proof, she looked to her side and found Ben sleeping soundly on his side of the king-sized bed. The bed had nothing to do with her insomnia. She had no one else to blame but the tall, chestnut-haired man that was Sarah's husband. She didn't deny that she was attracted to Victor, although, she would never admit it to Ben and most especially to Sarah. They were both married for Christ's sake! But she couldn't stop thinking about his deep, blue eyes, and the way he rubbed the back of his neck or adjusted his glasses when he was nervous. She could tell that Ben was a lot more confident than him, and usually Danielle would be turned off by that kind of show of insecurity. But, instead, it made Victor even more endearing to her.

She sat up slowly, so as not to wake her husband. She was craving her favorite bowl of cereal that she always relied on to take her mind off things. Hopefully, she'd fall asleep as soon as she was done. Tiptoeing, Danielle put on her pink silk robe and silently walked out of the room, closing the door gently behind her. When she looked up, she was shocked to find Victor standing in front of the fridge, looking inside with a frown. He wasn't wearing his glasses, but more importantly, he was topless.

The yellowish-light coming from the open fridge illuminated his rock-hard abs. His blue pajamas were riding low on his hips and Danielle could see the light trail of hair that started from his belly button and disappeared in his pajamas. 'Oh, there goes my heart again,' Danielle thought, putting a hand over her chest. Sure enough, her heart was beating rapidly against her palm.

Suddenly, Victor was looking at her, his blue eyes widening at the sight of her. "D-Danielle," he said, stuttering and looking utterly bewildered. "Have you been there long?"

Now, Danielle might be married to one of the hottest and most handsome man the world has ever produced, but she found Victor to be absolutely adorable. There couldn't be any harm with starting a conversation with the man. Maybe they could talk over a bowl of cereals.

"No, not really," she said, walking up to him and reaching down for the carton of milk. "I couldn't sleep so I thought I'd make myself a bowl of cereal." She turned around to get a bowl and started pouring milk and cereal. "Want some?" Danielle asked without looking at him. She heard him close the door of the fridge softly.

"Sure, I was feeling a bit peckish myself," Victor replied, pulling out chairs for them to sit on while Danielle prepared his cereal. "So...how long have you and Ben been married?"

"Almost three years," she replied, handing him the bowl and sitting beside him. "You and Sarah have been married longer, right?"

Victor didn't reply right away. He didn't really hear her question because of the fact that he was staring at her. The way the soft moonlight from the window illuminated her skin was almost magical that he couldn't look away. "I'm sorry," he said, licking his lips nervously. "I'm a bit distracted. What was that?"

"What's distracting you?" Danielle asked. She hadn't played this game in a long time; the game of flirtation and seduction. It was reasonable since she had been with the same man for three years. There was this air of almost child-like innocence around Victor that she couldn't resist. And as long as nothing really happened, everything was ok, right? No harm, no foul?

"It's just that...you're really beautiful," he shyly replied, his eyes looking down at his untouched bowl of cereal. "Ben's a lucky guy to have you."

The words touched her heart because Danielle knew Victor was being sincere and that this was no ploy for him to seduce her. She reached out to put a hand on his arm, and it twitched under her touch. "Thank you," she said, squeezing the arm lightly. "That's very sweet of you to say." And, before she could even stop herself, she moved closer and planned to kiss him on the cheek.

"What—," Victor, without intending to, turned to face Danielle at the last second and, for the first time ever, their lips brushed. Chills ran up their spines at the soft kiss and they looked at each other with wide eyes, an uncomfortable silence surrounding them both. Danielle stood up quickly, the chair almost giving way had she not caught it in time with her hands.

"It's getting really late," she said in a hurried voice, her eyes darting everywhere unable to look at Victor's face. "I..." she started to say, wanting to apologize. But she was too embarrassed now to say anything else. So, instead, she went back to her room as quickly as she could and closed the door behind her silently. She'd be in big trouble if Ben woke up after that incident.

Victor sat there, staring at the suddenly unoccupied chair beside him. He shifted his eyes to the pair of untouched cereal. "How the hell did that happen?"

## An Evil Plot

Ben had no idea about what happened between Danielle and Victor, but he was sure that something did happen. He could tell from the way Danielle moved; he had been married to her long enough for him to be able to read her like an open book. Victor was just as obvious. The man couldn't even look at his face without looking away with a frown on his face, and when Ben tried talking to him, Victor seemed intent on replying with one-liners, trying to end the conversation as soon as possible. Something was up, and although he figured he should probably be more concerned, he was surprised to find that he wasn't. He was too preoccupied with staring at Sarah's perky ass as she and Danielle played beach volleyball in their bikinis.

Sarah was truly sexy in her pink bikini.

He didn't know if she worked out on a daily basis or if she was just blessed with having a beautiful, statuesque body. She could give all the supermodels in the world a run for their money if she wanted to. Ben couldn't help but compare her to his wife.

Danielle was definitely attractive; with her big breasts and tiny waist, men couldn't help but gawk at her. Ben took pride in his wife because of her beauty and he loved her very much. But being married to the same person for three years was a feat for Ben who was notorious for being a playboy before he met Danielle. Sarah brought that out in him, and all he wanted to do was see her in all her naked glory. He wanted to spread those lithe, milky legs of hers and use his mouth and tongue on her until she was screaming his name in wanton abandon. He smiled at the image that made his cock twitch. If he wasn't careful, his cock would be jutting out and form a tent on his beach shorts. He looked to his right and noticed that he wasn't the only one staring at the two women; Victor was ogling them as well.

Ben furrowed his eyebrows. He looked back to the two women, when he realized that Victor wasn't staring at them both. He was only staring at Danielle. Ben smirked, a mischievous scheme forming in his head.

## Drunken Stupor

The vacation went by like a blur and before they even realized it, three days had gone by. They had done everything they could do in the span of three days from going on a city and country tour of the island, relaxing in a one-hour cruise, snorkeling, and going underwater in their own Scenic Underwater Bubble. Every night, after dinner, they'd go back to their suite exhausted and fall asleep right away.

Today, their last day of vacation, they were intent on just relaxing; a suggestion that was made by Ben. Everyone was surprised when he suddenly started suggesting plans left and right for their last day. So, relax they did. They made a trip to the hotel spa that afternoon, all four of them getting full body massages. The women stayed an extra hour longer to get their nails done, while Ben and Victor bonded over a game of billiards.

In the evening, they all went on a cruise that served a myriad of dishes from different cuisines. They momentarily forgot all the awkwardness and the pent up sexual frustrations they had been feeling for the past few days. That is, until they went to the local bar.

The mix of alcohol, laser lights, loud music, and dancing was so intoxicating that all the sexual energy they had been trying to keep at bay returned on full. And, because of the alcohol, none of them were feeling particularly shy anymore. They no longer bothered concealing their heated gazes and their partners didn't even notice because they, too, were preoccupied.

'What am I doing?' Sarah asked herself. She stopped dancing abruptly as she remembered who she was and that the guy she was having eye-sex with was not her husband. 'I need to snap out of this!' she berated herself as she reached out to pull Victor aside.

"Honey, let's go back," she shouted over the blaring music. Victor tilted his head so that he could hear what she was saying. "We've got an early flight tomorrow. Let's go back."

Danielle, who could make out what Sarah was saying, tugged on Ben's shirt. She agreed with Sarah and felt so guilty for what she did. Grinding on Ben, going lower and lower, while looking straight into Victor's eyes and giving him a hefty view of her chest was not something she was proud of. She had too much to drink tonight and it was time for them to go back to the hotel before she did something she would definitely regret.

The men begrudgingly agreed, dragging their feet and mumbling under their breath; making it apparent that they didn't want the night to end. But Sarah and Danielle wouldn't hear any of it and resolved to go to bed as soon as they were back in their suite.

"You girls go on ahead," Ben said with a silly grin on his face as soon as they were back in the hotel He threw an arm around Victor's shoulders. "Vic and I have unfinished business."

Danielle sighed and put her hands on her hips, looking sternly at her husband. "Baby, let's go to bed. Now," she said sternly.

It was Victor's turn to argue. "But we got unfinished business," he said a bit too loudly. His glasses were askew and his face was already red. "You and Sarah can go ahead," he added.

Sarah shook her head but opted to stay quiet. She turned around and went inside her room, motioning for Danielle to do the same. Her blonde friend cast one last dirty look at their husbands but said nothing else, and went inside her room as well.

It was around an hour later when Sarah heard the door to her room open. She hadn't been able to sleep because of all of the guilt that she felt and regret at having planned this whole vacation. But her trail of thought was broken when she felt a hand on her knee going higher and higher up her leg and inside the oversized t-shirt that she changed into earlier.

Sarah opened her mouth to tell Victor that she wasn't in the mood when her lips were suddenly too occupied to do anything but return a very heated kiss.

## Accidental Foreplay: Sarah

There was something different in the way Victor kissed her; an almost animalistic aura to it. He had never kissed her this way before, as if she was being dominated. The way he gripped her wrists above her head with one hand and tugged her panties down with the other, almost ripping the fabric apart, was so unlike the sweet, romantic husband that she knew. 'It's the alcohol,' she concluded, having never made love with Victor during the rare times he was drunk.

She moaned loudly when she felt his hand stroking the skin just above her pussy, sometimes moving to the sides to lightly brush over her nether lips, teasing her in the most torturous of ways. Sarah arched her back slightly, trying to goad him into moving his hand so that it touched her center. But, instead, he moved away, making her whimper at the loss of contact, to remove the only article of clothing left that she was wearing. She heard the shuffling of clothes before the sound of them being thrown to the side and then he was back with a vengeance; nipping her neck, deliberately scraping his teeth lightly on her skin. She could do nothing but moan and grip the headboard above her tightly as his lips went lower, capturing an unsuspecting nipple.

"Oooh," she moaned, unable to lower her voice. But his mouth was far from his final destination as it went even lower and lower until she felt two hands on her thighs, spreading them apart. There was no more dilly-dallying as she felt a tongue dart out to encircle her clit making her moan with ecstasy. He made it even worse by inserting a finger inside her, and expertly finding her pleasure button. She came without warning, her back arched and her toes curled.

She relaxed a few seconds later, still panting heavily. But as she felt his hard cock poking her thigh, she somehow knew that it was far from over.

### Accidental Foreplay: Danielle

Danielle had fallen asleep as soon as she changed into her silk baby doll. She had no idea how long the men bonded before she felt a pair of soft lips started kissing her neck gently, waking her up from her sleep. She blinked drowsily a few times, waiting for her eyes to adjust to the darkness, but she could hardly see anything; just a silhouette of a man.

"Ben?" she drawled, raising her hand to rub her eyes with the back of her hand. "What time is it?"

"Shhh," she heard him say, putting a finger to her lips before going back to kissing her neck. As she grew more aware of her surroundings, she noticed that her husband was acting differently from how he normally acted when they had sex. Normal sex with Ben was rough, almost violent. A far cry from the gentle kisses he spread throughout her face and neck. She also noticed that he was already fully naked, whereas she was still fully clothed. But that changed when he pulled the string that held her silk baby doll together, making her as naked as he was as she didn't bother putting on underwear that night.

His lips moved lower until she felt his tongue encircling her nipple, and the other being thumbed. She sighed blissfully from his ministrations and was glad that, for once, her nipples weren't sore from the little bites that he usually gave her. And then his lips and hand pulled away, making Danielle pout in the dark. She felt him straddle her torso and she knew what was coming next when he put his cock in the valley between her breasts.

Smiling, she put her breasts together with both of her hands, brought out her tongue and licked the tip of his cock, tasting a bit of pre-cum. Her smile grew wider when she heard him groan deeply in his throat. He moved his hips slowly at first, but speeded up after a few thrusts. She knew the exact moment he was going to cum and she latched he mouth on the head of his cock to catch his cum. Danielle moaned as the hot liquid hit her throat.

He was still hard even after he came and Danielle didn't have to guess what was coming next.

## Accidental Sex: Sarah

Sarah was still reeling from the last orgasm that she had when a hard cock entered her swiftly, a sound that was half a gasp and half a moan escaping from her lips. She felt him withdraw slowly until only the head was left and was shocked when he suddenly slammed hard right back into her. He started quickening his thrusts, but he was still fucking her hard, making her scream and writhe in a delicious mix between pain and pleasure.

He then maneuvered her so that she was face down, making sure to lift her ass high in the air; he did all of this while he was still inside her. Sarah couldn't believe that this was happening. She had never experienced this kind of lovemaking. This intensity was new to her, and she was having a hard time keeping up with Victor who, before this, always made love to her as if she was fragile and breakable. She decided that, although it was still strange, she liked how he was fucking her now with the hard thrusts and varying positions, the way he gripped her hips almost painfully, how he would subject her to his torturous kisses and touches. It was making her lose control, bringing out this uninhibited woman that she never even knew she was capable of being. She met him thrust for thrust until she came with such ferocity that made her head spin.

He chuckled and gave her ass a playful slap, something Victor had never done. She felt him lean forward until his chest was touching her back. "I'm not done with you yet," he whispered hotly in her ear sending shivers down her spine. He withdrew from her and lifted her up again so that they were facing away from the headboard with him directly behind her. When she realized what he had planned, she blushed hotly as she faced the full-length mirror that hung on the wall in front of the bed. He lifted her up and sat her down on his cock, granting Sarah a view of her in the mirror with her knees lifted up and spread wide. Her pussy was wet and it glistened from the little light from the window.

"Move," he whispered in her ear, his hand moving to her pussy to stroke her clit She blushed and moaned but did nothing to stop him. Watching herself in the mirror as she moved up and down his length was so incredibly erotic, Sarah didn't even recognize herself. She moved her hips faster, his moans sounded like soft growls in her ear, turning her on even more.

"Oh god, oh god, oh god," she moaned as she felt the pressure building and building until it exploded inside her. He came at the same time she did; a sharp groan escaping from his lips as he tightened his grip on her thigh.

They collapsed on the bed, exhausted with their lovemaking. Sarah smiled as she looked behind her to kiss Victor but stopped abruptly. It wasn't her husband who was in the room with her. It wasn't Victor who made her scream and writhe only minutes before, making her cum again and again.

Sarah closed her eyes, hoping that it was all a bad dream and that she'd wake up to reality as soon as she opened her eyes. But when she did, it was still a very naked Ben with her on the bed.

## Accidental Sex: Danielle

Danielle felt like a princess as he kissed her, gently coaxing her tongue to meet his. His touches were as light as feathers on her skin and she felt herself getting wetter because of it. He worshipped her body with soft licks and kisses as he rubbed her clit with his hand. She was slick and wet as he inserted two fingers inside of her. Everything he did to please her was done in soft and tantalizingly slow motions that made her slightly arch her back and moan in pleasure.

He moved and settled herself in between her spread legs and put his hard length inside her slowly, always slowly. Danielle was so used to the rough and fast sex that Ben always treated her with that she didn't think she'd love the slow and gentle lovemaking she never had, until now. But, oh, did she love it. She loved how he held her close and rocked her tenderly; putting his cock in and out of her, in, out, in, out. He captured her lips again with the same gentleness as Danielle put her arms around his neck in a way that made it seem as if she was making sure that he stayed there.

She could feel every inch of his cock inside her, hitting her deepest and most sensitive spots. She felt so loved and wished that this moment never ended. But it did, hitting her with pleasure rolling throughout her body. For the first time ever, she didn't come violently like she always did in the past. But that didn't make it less pleasurable, in fact, her orgasm lasted longer than it ever did and she couldn't help the tensing of her whole body as she moaned loudly against his soft lips. While she was cumming, he continued to move inside her, intensifying her orgasm.

He came after a short while and collapsed on top of her. She reveled at the feel of his body pressing down on hers as she hugged him tightly. He kissed her lovingly on her forehead before withdrawing his limp cock and lying down beside her as he held her close to him.

Danielle tensed, her eyes widening when she looked up at the face that she expected belonged to her husband. Instead, she was face-to-face with the chestnut-haired man who was the center of her attention these past few days: Victor.

## A Grave Mistake

Sarah got up from the bed, making sure not to wake Ben. 'How the hell did this happen?' was the question that Sarah asked herself over and over again. Her instincts were already telling her minutes before that something was wrong, that her husband was acting differently but she chalked it up as an effect to the amount of alcohol that he drank tonight. How could she have been so stupid? She berated herself again and again, as she put on the oversized tee that she was wearing. She hurried to the door, but when she opened it, she came face to face with a very tear-stricken Danielle.

It looked like she was about to knock on the door when Sarah opened it. "Sarah," she said, tears flowing freely from her eyes. "I'm so sorry."

Sarah led her to a chair; Danielle's sobs were growing louder by the second. As soon as she saw Danielle, she already had an idea what had happened and she tried hard to stop the tears that were threatening to fall.

"I'm sorry, too," she whispered, a bit surprised to find that her voice was hoarse. "Danielle, I didn't know it was Ben."

The blonde nodded in understanding, her hand flying to her mouth in an attempt to muffle her sobs. "What do we do?" she asked Sarah, her eyes wide with fear. "If Ben finds out—oh, Sarah. I don't want him to ever find out!"

Sarah rubbed her arm. "I know, I don't want Victor to know either." They fell into an uncomfortable silence that lasted for a few minutes. They were desperately thinking of a way to solve their dilemma.

They didn't want their husbands to know because they had no idea what would happen if they did.

"W-We could tell them that they accidentally fell asleep in the wrong room," Danielle said after a few moments. "We'd only be half-lying then. Anyway, they did enter the wrong room."

Sarah nodded. "And then we could say that we swapped rooms because they were so drunk?" she asked, wondering if that plan was actually plausible.

"Yeah, I think that could work," Danielle said. She looked up at Sarah and started crying again. "I'm so sorry, Sarah. I honestly didn't know! I swear I wouldn't have done it if—"

"Shh," Sarah interrupted her, putting a finger on Danielle's lips. "I know, and I'm sorry too. I don't know why I didn't notice that it was Ben."

They cried together, filled with regret, until the wee hours of the morning. They swapped rooms just as they had planned, and hugged their husbands as they wept softly, desperately wishing that all of this was just a bad dream.

### Secrets And Goodbyes

It was around nine in the morning when Ben and Victor started waking up from their slumber. Neither Sarah nor Danielle could sleep, and by the time the men woke up, everything was already packed and they were ready to go.

By eleven, they were already in the van that would take them back to their airport. The men were still chatting happily; seemingly oblivious to what had happened the night before. They didn't even notice that their wives were abnormally silent. And even if they did notice, none of them questioned the women.

There were times when Ben and Victor would talk about what they remembered after drinking and Sarah would tense. She and Danielle would subtly look at each other and supplied them with false information as planned, hoping that they would buy it. The men only nodded and went right back to talking amongst themselves. By four pm, their plane landed. And Danielle was eager to separate from the two.

"But we don't mind taking you back to your house," Victor said, looking at Danielle. The blonde looked everywhere but him. She settled on looking at Sarah.

"That's okay; we can take a cab from here. We're all tired and it'll be an even longer drive for you guys if you take us home, but thanks for the offer," she said, smiling nervously, hoping Sarah would convince Victor to just agree.

Ben shrugged. "Danielle's right. We appreciate the thought though, thanks man." He shook Victor's hand. "But let me at least help you load your luggage."

"That'd be great, thanks. I could use the help," and with that, the men walked to the car. It was a fairly safe enough distance for Sarah and Danielle to say their goodbyes.

"You know," Danielle said, looking at her feet. "You're a dear friend to me, Sarah. But I don't think we should see each other anymore, at least, not anytime soon."

Sarah nodded, saddened by the thought of not seeing her friend for another couple of years or so. But she understood the necessity of the long-term separation. "I know. I wish this vacation never happened."

They stayed silent after that, waiting for the men to finish. They had already finished with the luggage and were saying their own goodbyes.

Ben slapped Victor on the back. "So...I guess I'll be seeing you around."

Victor chuckled as he adjusted his glasses. "Definitely. I had fun, Ben."

"So...what did you think?" Ben asked, lowering his voice so only Victor could hear him.

"Danielle was a-m-a-z-i-n-g. I'd never had a woman with tits like hers," he replied, lowering his voice as well. He glanced at the women to see if they were looking at them but found that they were just looking at their feet. Victor didn't feel as guilty as he was supposed to feel. "And Sarah?" he asked.

Ben grinned. "A sweet, sweet pussy, my friend."

# AUTHOR'S NOTE

Readers: I want to expand a few of the stories to see where the characters can be explored further. If there are any of the stories that you would like to read more about again, I'd love to hear from you!

Visit my blog at www.breanakohr.com

Join my newsletter for free exclusive previews
www.breanakohr.com/in

Follow me on Twitter at
www.twitter.com/breanakohr

Like my page on Facebook at
www.facebook.com/breanakohr

Discover my books at major ebook retailers everywhere.